EVER WORLD

MYSTIFY THE MAGICIAN

K. A. APPLEGATE

SCHOLASTIC INC.
New York Toronto London Auckland Sydney
Mexico City New Delhi Hong Kong

FOR MICHAEL AND JAKE AND OUR LITTLE FRIEND MAISY

No part of this publication may be reproduced in whole or in part, or stored in a retrieval system, or transmitted in any form or by any means, electronic, mechanical, photocopying, recording, or otherwise, without written permission of the publisher. For information regarding permission, write to Scholastic Inc., Attention: Permissions Department, 555 Broadway, New York, NY 10012.

ISBN 0-590-87988-X

12 11 10 9 8 7 6 5 4 3 2 1   1 2 3 4 5/0

Printed in the U.S.A.

First Scholastic printing, January 2001

CHAPTER
I

The tongue was about the same size as me and it was determined to shove me under those grinding teeth.

I was too big a bite of pizza, too much *chalupa*. I was that bite you take out of the Big Mac when you're really starving, and you wish you could spit it back out and start over, but you can't because you have a yap full of gray meat and stale bread and you have no choice but to mash that puppy while the special sauce dribbles down your chin and makes you look like a two-year-old working his first solid food.

The tongue shoved at me, heaved up beneath me, all wet muscle covered in bristly taste buds the size of cashews. I was facedown on the tongue, facedown on a wet, pink blanket draped over half a dozen WWF stars trying to heave me off, push me, shove me, force me under molars as big as my head.

The roof of the giant's mouth came down, clamped me, forced the air out of my lungs, and the tongue tried to toss me again. I sucked air, sucked in his god-awful, stinking-like-a-week-old-corpse breath. The stink alone would have killed me if I'd had time to worry about it.

The tongue twisted me around. I was holding on with my hands slippy-gripping, my feet up against the rubbery inner cheek, calves lined up perfectly across the anvil of the lower jaw, just waiting for the downstroke. I felt the jaw contract, sensed rather than saw the mashers coming down, yanked my feet toward me, into a fetal position, crying for Mommy and getting a mouthful of giant spit.

Down came the teeth. I cleared them by a millisecond, but my convulsive movement had loosened my grip and now the tongue had me. It shot forward and sideways and I was on my back, big damned teeth sticking into my spine. I was lined up, gripped, held in place between tongue and cheek.

The mouth opened, just enough light to see the uppers coming down hard and fast, and instinct took over — I rolled, pushed at the yielding flesh of the cheek, like pushing against a half-inflated balloon. I shoved off the uppers as they came down, and suddenly, I was peanut butter: a big wad of weeping, yelling, peeing-myself peanut butter between teeth and cheek.

No way to breathe, the pressure of the cheek and gums was too much. And now the tongue was trying to dig me out, a freaking backhoe looking to dig a trench, and me in the role of the dirt.

I grabbed the digging tongue tip and yanked it over and past me. It slid down my face, my chest, and was gone. Any second now it was going to occur to the giant to use his finger. Or he could just slap the side of his face and I'd burst like a prom-night zit.

Panic. Sheer, no-brain, losing-it panic. I kicked, lashed out, slammed my fists in the confined space, buried alive and just waking up. Knees, feet, fists, head, and all-around writhing.

Something gave. I kicked and kicked, with a target now. I kicked and there came a bellow, reverberating up through the flesh and the gums and the bones and rattling through me before it burst full-fledged from the giant's mouth.

The tooth came loose. I gave a savage, blind kick and the whole molar rolled over onto the tongue. Blood gushed around me, blood and spit and the giant yelling and me yelling and mad now, mad because I'd had that tiny little impact that lets total save-me-Mommy despair give way to screw-you hatred.

I shoved my head into the gap and felt in the dark for the molar. I hefted the small boulder up and piled it on top of the nearest surviving tooth. Down came the uppers.

"Chew on that!" I screamed.

Crunch. And now a serious bellow and a gassing of manure-stinking breath and he slapped his cheek, slapped it and knocked me back out onto the tongue. I doubled up, legs numb from the blow, and kicked, unfeeling. I kicked with all I had, which wasn't much on the left side, where my leg was either broken or just numb. But my right foot caught the backside of a front tooth and knocked it spinning out into the air.

How many teeth in the giant mouth? Well, whatever that number was, minus two.

All at once I was falling. A long way. I hit ground and bounced. Head spinning, swirling, down and dark and . . .

At the top of my lungs I shouted a four-syllable word that was very popular with Eddie Murphy back when he was doing stand-up.

I shouted that word, jumped to my feet, spun, and fell into my girlfriend's mother. She was a small woman, and I carried her and her serving platter of lemongrass chicken right down to the geometric-pattern rug and lay on top of her panting like a sled dog in the last lap of the Iditarod.

There was a horrible silence. A silence so complete that of the four people in that tastefully decorated dining room with the matching antique table and sideboard and the table linen that was the same as that favored by the late Princess of Wales, I don't believe there was so much as the sound of a single heartbeat.

My girlfriend, Jennifer, my girlfriend for a week, said, "Christopher, I think you'd better go."

Up till that point I had not guessed that Jennifer had a talent for understatement.

Jennifer's father was not a big man; I had a good six inches on him. But the deep moral authority that comes to a man who has just stood by while someone screamed that particular Eddie Murphy word and then launched himself into the cleavage of said small man's wife as though determined to make that word a prophecy, well, a man in that position carries more than his natural height and weight.

I babbled an incoherent apology, tried to help the mother up, was grabbed by Jennifer, who literally shoved me toward the door while her father snatched up a silver candlestick and came after me.

I fled into the night and ran for my car with cries and shouts and shrill accusations following me.

Then I woke up, on my back, soaked with giant spit and tooth blood and stinking like the gym locker of the kid who left his sweats behind through the long months of summer vacation.

The giant loomed huge. His leprous, rotting, distorted, snaggle-toothed, malevolent-idiot face wore a dimly abashed expression.

"You okay?" David asked calmly.

Before I could work up a suitably savage reply, there came a woman's voice. A voice that was, literally, music.

"The poor boy, the poor boy," the voice said. "Oh, look at him, the pity of the world. There is the stream nearby. I will bathe him and tend his wounds with my own hands, poor, lovely young lad."

I wiped giant goo out of my eyes and sat up and looked at her. She was simply the most beautiful creature I have ever seen.

"I really *could* use a bath," I said.

Everworld.

Someday I hope to be able to book tours of the place. It'll be huge with borderline psychotics who don't get quite enough charge out of blind-folded extreme snowboarding, or who find handcuffed NASCAR too tame.

Everworld. Sure it's a place, but more than that: It's an idea! A really *bad* idea.

Way back in the day, way, way back before the discovery of toothpaste; back in the days when even the nicest folks were expected to maintain at least three distinct species of body vermin; way back in the glorious days of yore when you could be considered good-looking if the small-pox had gouged only pea-sized holes in your face rather than excavating craters the size of condi-ment cups; way back then, the gods of myth decided they'd had enough of Earth as we know it and wanted to set up a new home.

Why did they bail out on the real world? We don't actually know, but the best guess is that they were put off by the rampant sanity that was breaking out all over. You might not think of the darkest of the Dark Ages as being a riot of liberalism, what with plagues of the week; a lifestyle consisting almost entirely of backbreaking work, heavy drinking, and wife-beating; homes that were about as pleasant and sanitary as the kind of puppy-mill kennel that gets shut down by *60 Minutes;* and entertainment that involved the widespread killing of witches — and the even more widespread killing of chicks who somebody thought might kind of look like witches.

And yet it seems this all smacked of some kind of crazy feminist, socialist, NPR fund-raiser, vegan bran muffins, and grande lattes kind of thing to the gods of yore.

Zeus and Odin and Isis and Quetzalcoatl and the Daghdha and the whole panoply of divinely infantile personalities got together in a rare moment of unity and created Everworld. A universe apart. A universe where magic is real. A universe where the gods could be left alone to run things their way and keep *H. sapiens* in his place: kneeling, begging, and in some cases playing the role of the pig at the barbecue.

And all was fine. Oh yeah, it was a happy little asylum. Until outsiders began to crash the party. Riffraff. Other gods. Alien gods. Because, you see, madness is not a singularly human thing.

Alien gods — and their obligatory alien suck-ups, servants, and victims — began popping into Everworld and lowering the property values. But even that was cool because one thing you can say about pagan gods: They're pretty tolerant of one another. Hey, why not? There are plenty of virgins for everyone to feed to the flames.

And then the wrong guy walked in the door: Ka Anor. Ka Anor went too far even for the gods. He was way out of line. His deal was he ate other gods.

Ka Anor and his Hetwan hordes were messing with the basic constitution of Everworld, which holds, right there in the first amendment, that gods can screw with humans, but no one screws with the gods. Congress shall make no law allowing some alien creep to do to the gods what the gods did to humans.

The gods were outraged. Also scared. Real scared. So you'd imagine they might all unite to fight this new power. You'd think that, except that the gods are not necessarily the brightest bulbs on the Christmas tree. And what they lack in sheer stupidity they make up in shortsighted malice. Too many of the gods still think they're going to work old Ka Anor. Manipulate him. Use him to gain advantage.

Well, I've seen Ka Anor. And I've seen Zeus and Huitzilopoctli and Neptune and Hel and even Athena, who is pretty decent compared to most gods, and that bunch is as likely to manipulate Ka Anor as the local Methodist church's Little League team is to take the Yankees down four straight in the World Series.

Loki is actually the smartest of them in his own sick way: He just wants out. He wants out of Everworld and back into the real world. And he even has the way to do it: Senna, the witch, the gateway, a girl I once made out with back in the real world when I was still under the impression that she was just different and not *different*.

So, anyway, as long as we're awake in Everworld we're in Everworld. Of course we're also in the real world, carrying on with our staggeringly normal lives amid the SUV's and Pottery Barns and eighty-seven cable channels of Chicago's northern suburbs. When I fall asleep (or get knocked on the head by some freak-show nightmare) the Everworld me pops back into the real-world me to give real-world Christopher a CNN Breaking News update: "Dude! Guess what? Some freaking melted-candle-faced, snaggle-toothed, all-over-hairy giant just tried to Juicy Fruit your ass. Have a nice day."

Which sometimes causes you to scream unfortunate words and leap all over the woman your girlfriend will be in twenty years.

Anyway, so there are five of us if you count the witch, and I don't see how I can avoid counting her since she's the reason we're here without so much as a razor, a bar of soap, or a change of underwear.

David Levin is our Fearless Leader, our Ulysses S. Grant. He wants to grow up to be Russell Crowe in *Gladiator* but without the beard. He's our very own hero. The man with the sword — Galahad's sword, no less. The man with the great big stick up his hinder. David "no booze, no babes, no party" Levin. David of the perpetually gritted teeth and manly clenched jaw.

Don't get me wrong, I'm glad David's here. Hey, without him I'd be even more thoroughly and deeply screwed than I am. I'm still alive and bitching in large part because of General Davideus. But lord, the boy is a buzz-stomper.

Then there's Jalil. Jalil, whose motto is, "I'm smarter than you." Jalil, the only person I've ever known who actually did the extra-credit reading. Possibly the only person who has never slept in math class. He's a prickly, touchy, superior, arrogant, condescending butt-spasm, he really is, but I'm getting so I like him.

First and foremost because Senna hates him. Senna taunts and humiliates her half sister, April; she has contempt for me; she uses David like her own personal sock puppet; and all that's fairly normal for Senna. But she hates Jalil the way a Republican hates Bill Clinton. She hates him with the special hatred you reserve for someone who has slapped you around the parking lot in the past and may just do it again.

You have to admire that. You don't really hate what you don't really fear. Senna is afraid of Jalil for some reason, and the enemy of my enemy is my friend, as they say in all the really squalid, hopeless, self-destructive corners of Earth.

Finally, among the "normals" there's April. As much as Senna, shall we say, dislikes Jalil, that's how much April can't stand her half sister. April is sunshine to Senna's overcast, nice to her nasty, Ben Kenobi to her Anakin.

She's a babe: about five cubic feet of lose-yourself-in-it red hair; the kind of wise, confiding, I'm-in-on-the-joke green eyes that give you the feeling that, hey, what the hell, give it a shot, she'll let you down easy.

She's a wanna-be actor. A people collector. A friend magnet. A rare example of a person who can be religious and moral and all that without making a happy, decadent, self-serving swine like me want to choke her.

April loves to bust me. I love to be busted by her. There's absolutely no chance we'll ever be a couple. And yet, optimist that I am, I figure to keep giving it a shot.

Figured on that, up until the point when I saw Etain. That was her name. Etain.

Chapter

III

After our water-breathing adventure in Atlantis we had washed up on a scruffy little beach of dark sand and gnarled driftwood, overhung by low bluffs beneath a glowering dark sky. The bluffs were cut by a brook that ran right into the sea carrying no great amount of water.

We climbed the bluffs, something the giant did in one big step, and found ourselves in a lumpy, rolling landscape of stunted trees and mossy rocks. There were sheep grazing nearby. There were stone fences that looked more picturesque than functional. In the distance I saw a suggestion of a castle, a hint of a village.

Etain led us up and over the damp, springy grass to a bend in the brook.

I did not let Etain bathe me. Give me some

credit. I'm not a complete dog. Besides, David wouldn't let me.

But I let her show me where the stream formed a deep, still pool. A big elm tree, not too different from the one in my own front yard, but unique in this landscape, grew tall beside the brook. The pool was so still, so mirror-smooth that the tree was reflected in perfect detail.

I nervously stripped while everyone ostentatiously turned away, and waded into water so cold it should have been solid, all the while resisting the illusion that I was really plunging into the branches of an inverted tree.

Etain took my filthy clothes and rinsed them and slapped them on the rocks and rinsed them again and slapped them and finally hung them from a low branch.

Which left me standing waist-deep in arctic runoff and wondering what happened if half your body Popsicled.

Etain noticed my predicament, me shivering and clutching myself. She laughed her laugh and I smiled and Jalil smiled and April smiled and even David smiled. She had that kind of laugh.

Senna did not laugh. Senna doesn't laugh a lot.

Etain unwound a shawl from her shoulders and handed it to me, careful not to let it get wet. I did a nonchalant exit that involved advancing up out of the water while simultaneously adjusting the shawl lower and lower, all the while trying to look as cool as 007 in his tuxedo.

The giant was still there, still looking huge and scabby and a little sheepish, like a kid caught feeding his broccoli to the dog. Clearly the giant was under Etain's control. That fact made me pause. She was hot, Etain was, a red-haired, blue-eyed, creamy-skinned honey in a long, green, low-cut dress that showed more than a Victoria's Secret bra model bending over to pick up a quarter. But at the same time, this was Everworld, and this girl had a thirty-foot giant tugging at his forelock and digging his toe in the dirt.

"Lorg is very sorry to have swallowed you up the way he did," Etain said to me. "Apologize to the boy, then, Lorg."

The giant thought that over. Not as if he was deciding whether or not to obey, but rather as if it just took a while for the words to sink down into his brain, and longer still for him to figure out what they meant, and what he should do about it.

But at last he said, "Most humble apologies, sir." And to everyone's amazement he actually stuck out one leg and executed an arm-sweeping bow. And what could I do but bow right back?

People bow to you, it just brings out the counter-bow, like it or not.

"I hopes his honor ain't too discommoded?" the giant rumbled, his hideous face a mask of hideous concern.

"Who, me? Nah. I'll probably wake up screaming every night for the rest of my life, but hell, Lorg, I was doing that anyway. No hard feelings."

"There, and that was generous, wasn't it, Lorg?" Etain said pleasantly.

"I take it most kindly," the giant agreed with another bob of his big old rodeo-bull-sized head.

"They are an impetuous people, the Fomorii giants," Etain explained. "They are charged now with defending the land from invaders. Of course they are meant to deal with Vikings and Saxons and the like, not helpless, pitiful, shipwrecked souls."

"Where are we?" David asked. His sword was still drawn, held point down, but not sheathed.

"Do you not know?" Etain laughed. "This is the home of the Tuatha De Danann. The sacred isle of the Daghdha. 'Tis upon the blessed shores of Eire you've landed."

"Ireland?" April blurted.

"Ireland," Etain agreed happily.

"Hey, my name's O'Brien. My family is from Ireland. A long time ago, I mean. You know, dur-

ing the potato famine and . . . you know, came to
America . . ." April petered out as it occurred to
her that she was talking about an Ireland that had
never existed as far as the people of this Ireland
were concerned.

"I'm Jalil Sherman. I'm not Irish," Jalil said
dryly. "But I'm very pleased to meet you."

"David Levin," David said, sticking his hand
out. Etain looked a bit mystified, and after a moment David withdrew the hand and gave a kind
of jerky, embarrassed lurch that was supposed to
be a bow.

Etain didn't seem terribly impressed with David
one way or the other. But then she spotted his
sword and her eyes went soft and sad.

"So it's true, then. Galahad has fallen."

"Yes," David confirmed. "He gave me his
sword."

"We had heard rumors, but no one would believe it. The king will call for a week of mourning," she said. "Galahad was a hero to heroes. He
and the king were friends of old. So many brave
and good men have gone. Who is left to show us
the way in a dark world? And may I know this
lady's name?"

She gave Senna a cool up-and-down, not
hostile but wary, watchful. She sensed something
wrong about Senna.

"Senna Wales," Senna said, rushing to cut me off before I could say something snide.

"And I'm Christopher Hitchcock. I'm only Irish on Saint Patrick's Day." This was an idiotic joke, of course, but it was all the joke I had on me at the time. Try being funny when you're standing naked in a wet shawl under the concerned, if off-kilter, gaze of a giant. Ain't easy, my friend.

Etain felt my clothes. No way they could be dry, of course, but then she said, "They're dry," and I'd been in Everworld long enough to know that there's no point protesting the impossibility of things.

I got dressed and felt better about life. I gave Etain back her shawl, which, again, should have been damp at least but instead was as warm and fluffy as a towel straight from the dryer.

"You must join us for dinner," Etain said.

"You and Lorg?" Jalil asked.

Etain laughed her infectious, impossible-to-ignore laugh. "Lorg must stay here. The giants are not allowed in the town for fear that they may inadvertently do harm. No, you must dine with me in my father's house."

Senna said, "We are in a bit of a hurry. We have to make our way back to Olympus, we are . . . we are on a quest." She reached to touch Etain, a sort of girl-grab, you know, an innocent just-us-

girlfriends kind of touch. Of course I knew why
Senna was getting physical. We all did. Senna's
powers work better when she has direct physical
contact with the person she's trying to manipulate.

There was a blur. Several blurs actually. One
dropped from the tree above. One zipped out from
behind a rock outcropping. The other, I swear,
came straight up out of the stream.

In about the time it takes to think, *Whoa!* there
were three fairies standing, quivering, vibrating,
short bows drawn, arrows fitted, points leveled at
Senna, eyes squinting along the shafts with such
perfect concentration that you just knew they
were deciding on which exact ventricle they were
going to skewer.

We'd dealt with fairies before. Real fairies aren't
exactly the cute, cuddly, quaint little folks you
may have in mind. They're little, but not toy-
poodle little, or hamster little. More like twelve-
year-old-boys little. And fast, serious, smart,
dangerous boys. I guess some are technically leprechauns, but mostly I had the impression that
so-called leprechauns, all dressed up in the curly-
toed shoes and red caps, were an act for tourists.

Senna's hand stopped moving. Hung there in
the air.

And Etain let the moment drag on for just a bit longer than strictly necessary. She smiled the whole time, and her eyes were still lit from within, happy, carefree, but with just the tiniest bit of sharp steel glinting back behind all that Irish maiden charm.

"Now, now, good fellows, you are too careful by half," Etain said to the fairies. "Unbend your bows: Surely the creature means no harm to the daughter of the king."

The fairies gave off the same kind of relaxed, friendly, trusting vibration you get from Secret Service agents: It didn't matter what Etain said — if Senna had so much as farted, the fairies would have turned her into a pincushion. I'd seen fairies in action: They could reload while the first arrow is still flying.

Senna pulled her hand back very slowly.

The fairies were gone as fast as they'd appeared. It was like they'd never been there.

"Come, I will show you the way," Etain said. "The blackberries are ripe and the bushes groan with the weight of them. Let us fill our aprons!"

She set off, walking and skipping like a kid and leaving the five of us to follow in a more galumphy way.

Jalil sidled up beside me and gave me one of

his sly looks. "I think she likes you, man. Be bold:
Make your move. Skip on up there and hold her
hand. Grab a little squeeze."

He seemed to find this very amusing.

I looked around for the fairies. I couldn't see
them. But they were there. Oh yeah, they were
there.

CHAPTER

IV

By this point in my Everworld experience I'd seen a few things. And I'd been a few places: Loki's castle, Huitzilopoctli's bloody pyramid, Fairy Land, Olympus, Neptune's version of the submarine ride at Disney World, an upside-down African afterlife, and the foul, evil place occupied by the aptly named Hel. Lots of places.

So I was ready for anything. Anything except something so normal it made all of us stop dead in our tracks.

"That's a telephone pole," April said.

"Telegraph, I imagine," Jalil said.

"Ah, yes, that is the newest thing," Etain said. "It is quite fascinating. The wire is made of very thin copper. The spirit called electricity — the selfsame force that creates the lightning in a storm — the electricity runs along the wire faster than a fairy. By stopping and starting the flow of the electrical spirit one can speak, after a fashion, in a sort of simple code."

No one had anything to say to that at first. There was a sort of awkward, guilty silence. We had been the ones to introduce the telegraph to Everworld. We'd done it as part of an elaborate and desperate scheme to secure April's freedom from the fairy king and queen. They had been under the impression that she was Senna, the gateway, and were ready to sell her to Ka Anor. And of course, this being Everworld, there was a dragon involved.

But that had all happened maybe two, three months ago. And already there were telegraph wires going up in Ireland, an island presumably some distance from Fairy Land.

We exchanged looks. Our usual routine was to try and pass ourselves off as traveling minstrels. We sucked as minstrels, but we were more than good enough for the shockingly low standards of Everworld, a place without so much as a Christina or a Britney or a single Backstreet Boy, let alone any real entertainment.

Our strained silence did not exactly slip by Etain; she was looking expectant and attentive. David finally gave a kind of shrug. "Tell her," he directed Jalil.

"We made the telegraph in Fairy Land," Jalil said, swelling a bit with the pride of authorship.

"Did you?" Etain's eyes lit up. She grabbed Jalil's arm and stepped into him. "Then you are the ones! You are the ones!"

She put her hand to her mouth, as amazed as if she'd just seen the Pope standing in line at Wendy's.

"Yeah, we're the ones," I said, not willing to let Jalil soak up all the glory as the Great Telegrapher or whatever.

Of course it did occur to me — a bit too late — that we had left Fairy Land on bad terms. We'd pretty much threatened to get our dragon friend to barbecue the place. We'd been invited to leave and not come back unless we were interested in stopping a large number of fairy arrows.

"Of course what we really are is minstrels," I added.

Etain was nodding, looking very shrewd, looking not at all like the sweet, bouncy, good-time girl I'd taken her for. She paid particular attention to Senna. She didn't say anything, but I was pretty sure she now knew who and what Senna was. Etain did a little gesture with one finger held down by her side. A very small gesture.

I couldn't prove it, of course, I couldn't see it,

but I had the feeling Senna had just become target number one for a lot of taut-drawn bows.

Everyone else must have had the same feeling because as we moved on, there was a definite safe distance between Senna and the rest of us.

"Fios and his druids will be desperate to get at you," Etain said as we walked along the pleasant pathway under the shadow of the telegraph poles. "You must not let them keep you up all night with questions."

"The druids?" That didn't sound great.

"But, of course, you know nothing of our land," Etain said. "You are strangers. I am sorry, my wits are astray: I have never met prophets before." She laughed, but not sarcastically. She meant that "prophets."

"We're prophets?" April asked uneasily.

"Surely. You have brought wonders and revelations from the old world. You are bringers of knowledge and enlightenment. You are already much admired in this realm, though I'm afraid your names and even your descriptions have become sadly garbled in the retelling."

"Yeah?"

Etain laughed her laugh and said, "Oh, yes, you are described as beings of light, barely human at all, nor elfin, nor of any known race, but fantastically arrayed, fabulously tall, and bedecked

entirely with diamonds and rubies, with dragons
at your beck and call."

"That all sounds pretty accurate," I said.

Jalil said, "We haven't noticed that most of
Everworld exactly embraces new ideas."

"No," Etain agreed sadly. "The old gods fear
change."

"Don't you have any old gods?"

"Of course we do," Etain said. "Though, of
course, we've lost the dear old Daghdha. Eaten by
the beast Ka Anor."

"Yeah, we heard something about that," I said.

"We have all the old gods, the Tuatha De
Danann, bless them, but we also have the druids,
and the fairy folk, and my mother's own people,
the elves. And after the Great Bloodletting that
pitted gods and man against elves, fairies, and
druids, came the time of the Peace Council. And
since then we have had the blessings of peace."

"How long ago was that?"

"Oh, it has been two hundred and nine years
since the Peace Council met at the Magh
Tuireadh."

"That's amazing," April said. "Great, I mean.
It's pretty rare for people to be able to make peace
and stick to it."

"It's rare that any land is blessed with the wis-
dom and fortitude of a great man of vision. And

him a stranger to the land, too. Our shame is that we did not find the path to peace by our own efforts alone, but our glory is that once shown the way, we stayed true. We still hew to Merlin's way."

Senna stopped. Like her feet had been nailed to the ground. Etain noticed but kept walking. She nodded very slightly, acknowledging something she'd guessed.

"Merlin?" April said, unable to resist gloating at Senna. "Merlin the wizard?"

"There is only one Merlin the Magnificent," Etain said. She swept her hand around the horizon, encompassing the town, the ridge ahead, and the surrounding hills. "All of this is Merlinshire, my father's kingdom. And you" — her eyes narrowed, her face flushed — "you are the ones. The prophets from the old world. What transforming wonders may you teach us?"

It wasn't a question, more like a meditation. I could see the wheels turning in her brain. The more she thought about it, the deeper the pink in her cheeks. She was stoked for our knowledge. Kind of made me wish I had some.

Not that I wasn't busy thinking. I was thinking about the word *décolletage*. I'd read it somewhere, had no idea how to pronounce it. But it was preoccupying me right at that moment. I was pretty sure I should be doing some deep thinking about the significance of all this quasi-Ireland, of a place where science was welcomed, where they'd embraced the telegraph, where we were some kind of prophets. And yet, I was mostly focused on décolletage. And on the graceful line of her neck. And on the color of her hair.

I'm a fairly simple creature after all, just a happy dog. I like to think of myself as the human representation of a Reverend Horton Heat lyric.

And yet, simple as I am, I was pretty sure I was in love.

CHAPTER

V

The telegraph line followed the road and the road followed the stream. The stream issued from the spillway of a wooden dam. Behind the dam was a reservoir maybe a quarter mile in diameter and lined with parks and walkways, like the Lake Michigan waterfront by the university. I expected to see in-line skaters and bikers and running mommies pushing running strollers.

Meanwhile, the ocean shoreline had cut back to bring the sea up to the town, so that it now appeared we'd been walking along a bluff-lined peninsula. Behind the town the land grew rugged, sweeping up toward not-very-distant hills of bare stone and few trees.

The town was a port, a picture-perfect, neat little port with a wharf and stone piers and small, brightly colored fishing boats. The town seemed almost squeezed between the port and the man-made reservoir so that it had, in effect, two waterfronts, one wild and one like a park.

Past the town, across the park was a smaller, rockier promontory. And atop this bare, ugly protrusion was a virtual forest of windmills. All were faced away from us, turning in a wind we barely felt in our sheltered position. Poles ran to the windmills and carried wires back to the town, presumably to power the telegraph.

The town itself was constructed mostly out of lichen-stained limestone. Some buildings were plastered and whitewashed or painted in various watery colors. The roofs were thatch or slate. The streets were cobblestone and resounded with the clatter of shod hooves and iron-rimmed cart wheels.

Beyond the town itself, where the rocky promontory melded into a low, ominous ridge, there stood a castle. It had three towers, two smaller ones and one quite a bit larger. All were crenellated and connected by crenellated walls. It was pure, hard-core medieval-fantasy land, except for the fact that a number of very long, very bright pennants flew from staffs atop the tallest tower. And the fact that bright lights shone from every tall, narrow window.

It was eerie. The clouds hung low, the sun had

either set or was thinking seriously about doing so, and the gloom was as heavy as a November Monday. But piercing through it all, there were these lights.

"That is not candlelight," Jalil said.

He said it out of Etain's hearing.

"Looks like lights. Like regular lights, I mean," I agreed.

"Electric lights. Not in the town, though. See? Those are all dim, flickery: fire or candles."

Etain led us around the edge of the reservoir and at last into the town itself, past bakeries and butcher shops and cheese shops and stables, all of them closing down, shuttering for the night.

What few people were walking the streets seemed happy enough but in a hurry to get home. Commuters, I guess. But all who saw Etain took a second to smile and give a little bow, which she returned with grace.

They weren't scared people. That much I could figure out all on my own. They weren't like the poor losers trapped in Hel's aboveground harem, or the starving residents of Huitzilopoctli's sunny city. There was a complacent normalcy about them. They showed respect for Etain, and real affection, and from time to time a certain appreciation for décolletage.

"The streets are clean," Jalil pointed out. "Look: trash cans."

Normally not an earthshaking thing, but in Everworld cleanliness was next to nonexistent. Streets tended to be six inches deep in animal droppings. But not here.

My foot caught on something. A cobblestone. No. Not a cobblestone. I looked down and stared and grabbed April, who happened to be the closest person.

"Is that a train track?"

"Yeah. I noticed. Trolley. Or streetcar, or whatever. And by the way, look out."

It came up behind us, clattering, rattling, and now ringing a cheerful little bell.

"Rice-a-freaking-Roni," I said. It was a cable car. Like San Francisco. Just like with regular real-world cable cars there was a cable — hence the name — that ran underground and pulled the car up or down the street. I knew this because I'd been to San Francisco doing a little preliminary college survey. What powered the cable I didn't know, but it wasn't hamsters. And more to the point, it wasn't magic.

Of course the Everworld Irish had different ideas about how a cable car should look. This was more oval than rectangular, and done up in gold scrollwork and painted inset panels showing chubby babes being chased around fountains by grinning satyrs. The seats all faced out and were ornately carved fantasies with lions' heads and dragons' tails.

The car was full of passengers, most looking self-conscious and uneasy, but some looking very much like tired, yawning city workers coming home on the METRA. (Minus the briefcases, laptops, and cell phones.) The cable car was new, but not so new that it wasn't a big ho-hum to some of the riders.

There were four "crew": a brakeman, a guy who apparently just rang the bell, and two guys who rode standing at the back and as far as I could tell did nothing. All four were dressed like Elton John visiting the Renaissance Fair.

It was one hell of a cable car.

Jalil's eyes were lit up like a kid with his first PlayStation. He was chuckling to himself as he walked. Chuckling and muttering like some street crazy.

"Don't get too happy," I said. "It's still Everworld."

"Electric lights. Telegraph. Cable cars. Sanitation. It may be Everworld still, but as far as I'm concerned, I've figured out where to buy a condo."

We trailed along behind the cable car, which

eventually reached a wide, well-groomed town square: trees, a fountain, lawns, trimmed bushes, and in one corner, a stone commuter built beside a massive turntable used for rotating the cable cars. More commuters: humans, elves, fairies — though why a fairy would ride when he could just go zoom, I didn't know. Most of the humans wore the kind of stuff you would find at any medieval JCPenney: rough wool pullover deals, long leather shirts gathered with a belt, leg warmers, lace-up boots, limp caps, aprons. But the clothes were cleaner than usual, and the male faces generally had no more than a three-day growth. Unless they had beards, but even then it wasn't the Grizzly Adams, beard-that-ate-my-face look. Dentistry still wasn't all it might be — it was a rare grin that didn't make you wince to look at it. And the haircuts were the kind of thing you get at SuperCuts when the hairdresser is hungover.

One of the waiting commuters was different. He wore a long, layered robe, darkest blue over a lighter blue with a tease of creamy white. His boots were knee-high Mercedes upholstery leather. He had a large medal around his neck and a Lake Forest society lady's ring on his finger.

He wasn't old, but he seemed like he ought to be. He had a fine gray beard going but his skin was unlined, and he stood tall and strong and sure of himself. He watched us closely and met Etain's eye and gave her a nod. Then he slipped away from the crowd and disappeared from sight.

"Who's that, Gandalf?" I asked.

Etain gave a polite frown, like she was pretty sure I was being witty but wasn't getting the joke. "That was Darun the Younger."

"Was that a druid?" Jalil asked.

"Yes, certainly," Etain said. "I hope you are not one of those who harbor a foolish suspicion and even dread of druids?"

"Me, no," Jalil said. "I've never met one."

"Strangers sometimes hold foolish, fanciful notions of the druids," Etain said. "They are said to be wizards, magicians, even demons, and usually malicious. Some superstitious creatures even speak of human sacrifice, as though such a thing were even possible in this blessed land."

"Glad to hear that," I said. "We're deeply opposed to human sacrifice, what with being humans and all. So druids are not bad guys?"

"Certainly not. After all, I am a druid. Do I seem to be malicious? Threatening?"

"You're a druid?" I said stupidly, not sure what it might mean. What was that, like a nun or something?

"Surely, a Druid of the Green, though barely better than a novice. The Druids of the Green are concerned with the land, with trees and stones and all living things. The Druids of the Blue are concerned with learning, with scrolls and books and medicine. The Druids of the Red are advisers to kings and to ambassadors abroad. The Druids of the Black follow the stars and the seasons. And now, of course, we have the new order: the Yellow."

"Don't tell me: Druids that handle technology?"

Etain was intrigued. "Technology? What is the meaning of that word?"

I jerked my finger at Jalil and said, "Jalil? She wants to know what technology is."

"Technology refers to science with a practical application," he explained. "The telegraph, for example."

"Yeah. What he said," I agreed.

"Technology," Etain said, savoring the word. "Technology."

It gave me a chill. I'm not Jalil. I'm not some nerd. I'm not all that in love with the real world. I'm not some Palm-Pilot-tapping, beeper-wearing, Web-surfing, cell-glued-to-my-head techie. My love for technology is about cars and remote controls, that's about it.

But lord, to wander through the horror show of Everworld all this time, stumbling from one nightmare into the next, day after day of life as the gods have dictated it, man, that word, that clumsy, clunky word spilling from the luscious lips of that hottie, I don't know, it made me want to cry. I swear to God, I had tears in my eyes.

Technology. One word that summed up central air-conditioning and hot water and escalators and The Flaming Lips cranked up in your headphones and automatic transmissions and HBO and down-loadable bootleg term papers and beer that's really, really cold even on a hot day.

Technology. It was like the words *Snickers bar* to a starving man.

And that was just me. Poor Jalil thought he was at Disney World. We were all happy. All relieved. All but Senna.

Screw Senna, I thought. *If she's bummed, so much the better.*

Which was foolish: Even in the land of the Yellow Techie Druids you don't want to mess with a witch.

CHAPTER
VI

Etain's father was King Camulos, and he was a happy, red-faced, turnip-nosed, gray-haired old gent with a room-filling laugh that inevitably ended in a hacking cough. May have had something to do with the fact that he kept a fat stogie stuck in the corner of his mouth, even while eating and drinking.

I liked him right away.

Etain's mother, Goewynne, was a different story. She was an elf. We'd seen elves here and there but had never really spoken to one.

I guess I'd assumed they were just slightly bigger versions of fairies. But fairies are tolerably unmysterious creatures: They like to make money, they take no crap, and you always got the feeling with fairies that while they wouldn't enjoy killing you, they'd sure as hell do it in a hurry if they thought it was a good idea. If fairies ever break through into the real world you'll find them all within a few blocks of Wall Street.

But Goewynne was not a fairy. She managed to look as young as her daughter, as if no ray of sun had ever touched her cheek, as if no split end had ever dared to insult her tumbling, lustrous, diamond-dusted black hair, as if her hands had been eternally gloved in satin and never touched a rough surface.

She was beautiful in the way a Rolls Royce is beautiful: perfect, flawless, rich, and way beyond your reach, but you don't get the hormone rush you get looking at a cherry-red Viper.

She wasn't cold. Not really. She wasn't anything but charming and welcoming and gracious to a degree that would make Martha Stewart seem like a ragged, PMSing diva by comparison.

And yet . . . there were those eyes of hers. Palest blue. Iceberg blue. Million-year-old, seen-it-all, X-ray eyes. Not-impressed eyes.

If Etain and I got married, me and her dad could go to Cubs games, trade jokes, barbecue up some ribs in the backyard, and call each other Cam and Chris. Mom and I would be on a "yes, ma'am, no, ma'am," basis. She was one of those people you feel like you'd better salute or bow to. I did a little of both, just to be on the safe side.

We had an intimate little dinner, just us, Etain, Mom and Dad, and the druid named Fios who didn't smile, didn't talk, and barely ate or drank.

There were fairy guards and fairy waiters and a couple of crude electric lights like something out of Frankenstein's lab: arcs of snapping blue augmenting the candles.

We ate with forks and knives and spoons. There were napkins. No one threw their food on the floor. Only the king picked his teeth with a knife — all the while keeping his glowing cheroot in place. But the food was good enough and, to April's relief, included heaps of fresh green vegetables among the numerous overcooked animals.

There was good wine and I indulged, ignoring David's puckered disapproval. Old King Camulos and I got pretty toasted, followed at some distance by April and Jalil. The elf queen drank the wine but it might as well have been water. There was no "thaw" button for Mom.

"Etain tells us that you were present at the final battle of Galahad," Goewynne said at one point.

"Yes," David answered. He was about to say more, but with Goewynne you automatically felt like a defendant being cross-examined by a district attorney looking to get the death penalty, and your lawyer had instructed you not to volunteer information.

"We had guessed as much, yet it is bitter news," Goewynne said. "He was the perfect knight."

"Yes, yes," King Cam said, taking a deep swig around his cigar. Then his eyes lit up and he started grinning and chuckling in anticipation of tossing off a funny line. "Though I'd always thought our wedding night was the perfect night!" As he reached the last couple of words he broke up, gasping out the punch line, and then hacking like a cat with a hairball.

Goewynne produced an affectionate smile that kind of made me like her more. And it made me think the old king must have something going on to keep the elf queen happy.

When King Camulos was done wheezing he said, "I once fought Galahad, you know. Only a joust, and with blunted swords, but what a warrior! He stove one of my ribs in with the pommel of his sword and damn me if I didn't have him by the hair. We ended up rolling in the mud and laughing so hard we couldn't go on." He shook his head. "Ah, we'll have to declare a fortnight of mourning. A pity. Galahad would never approve: He wasn't one for crying over spilt blood."

I started to laugh, figuring that was a play on words, but Old Cam had misted up and was wiping his eyes with the back of his sleeve, so I stifled myself.

"You are from the old world," said a previously unheard voice. Fios. The druid. Maybe the boss druid, I didn't know for sure.

"Yes, we are," David answered him.

"How is it you come to be among us?" Fios asked. He reminded me of Merlin, only Merlin without the temper or the snippy impatience with fools. And he was younger. He wore a long, layered robe that revealed three different shades of yellow. Very tasteful, nothing too garish. He was clean-shaven, with a long, kind of horsey face and sad eyes.

David didn't hesitate. "We don't know how we came to be here," he lied.

Maybe Old King Cam bought that but Fios didn't and Etain didn't and Goewynne sure as hell didn't. But they were all polite enough about being lied to.

David dug the hole deeper, as poor liars often do, by offering more detail. "One moment we were there, then suddenly we were here. Not here in Ireland, here in Everworld. Viking country, actually. And since then we've been traveling. We actually were just in Atlantis. Actually, we're trying to get back to Olympus because we've been trying to help the gods there fight Ka Anor."

"Try not to use more than a dozen 'actuallys' in a sentence," I muttered. The boy was a pitiful liar.

There was an embarrassed silence while the elf queen and the half-elf princess and the druid all pretended not to notice that we were full of crap, and while we pretended not to know that they knew we were full of crap.

At last Etain spoke up. "Visitors who reach our shores are most often very happy to remain with us. And visitors such as yourselves, why, you would be honored guests. You have so much to teach us, and we honor learning in my father's kingdom and throughout the land. You would want for nothing: food, drink, pleasant lodging, servants, companionship."

"Sounds good to me," I said. I met her gaze and did my best to project sincerity, not something I do well. "This is the greatest place we've seen in Everworld. Nicest people, too. The most beautiful ladies." I nodded in a terrifically courtly, knightly sort of way, at Etain and at Mom. As smooth as I am capable of being.

Etain's smile was perfectly poised between vast amusement and sincere gratitude. Goewynne looked at me as if she'd just discovered that I wasn't a human at all, but a chimpanzee wearing pants.

The dinner wore on to a close with all of us talking pleasantly and dishonestly. Fios expressed the hope that real-worlders would get together with him and some of his boys the next day, and we agreed. We agreed because Goewynne very graciously endorsed the idea, and none of us wanted to find out what happened if you blew off the elf queen.

Plus, it seems, Etain was going to be there, too. And as far as I was concerned, I was going anywhere she was going.

CHAPTER

VII

I don't know, maybe it was just time for me to fall in love. I'd been through some changes. I'd gone from being a fairly normal kid wondering how to get into a college a long, long way from home, to being the official punching bag of the gods.

I'd seen things I wasn't going to soon forget. I'd seen the poor, doomed, tortured men in Hel's underworld. And I'd seen humans marching up an Aztec pyramid like so many cows on their way to the big Oscar Meyer package in the sky. I'd seen Ka Anor himself, that nasty piece of work, seen him eat a sweet, handsome poof named Ganymede who'd never done any harm to anyone.

Regular life had sucked, but it had sucked in the usual, barely tolerable ways: School was a joke, my parents were drunks, and life was pretty much centered around my couch, my remote, and Nick at Nite.

Now life sucked in color. It sucked in stereo. This was true broadband suckage, the suckage of the future, a whole new world of suckery. People were trying to kill me. Lots of them. Not out of any special malice toward me, it wasn't personal, it was just that whether it's Amazons or Aztecs or trolls or mermen or fairies or Hetwan or . . . well, one way or the other they had the one thing in common: an inexplicable desire to kill me.

So, yes, doctor, it has been a stressful time in my life. Prozac? Sure. I'll take a truckload.

Maybe that was it, maybe it was a reaction to stress, you know? My own tiny life force reaching out for something to hold on to. And Etain was something to hold on to. You know why? She laughed and even David couldn't help but laugh along. She was beautiful and she was smart and she had a sense of humor, and yes, she had a nice body, but honest to God that wasn't it.

It wasn't her body I was seeing as I lay there in the dark on a comfy bed with a fire slowly dying in the stone hearth. It was her face. Now that has to be love, right? You're thinking about a girl's face and laugh and movement and hair color and eyes and all that usually irrelevant stuff?

Stress. There's no other explanation.

But I didn't want to go to sleep. It had been a long day, what with escaping from the bottom of the freaking ocean and being some giant's Juicy Fruit, but I didn't want to sleep because if I slept I'd slip across to the real world. And over there the other Christopher, the one who hadn't seen Etain up close, the cynical, smart-ass Christopher untouched by love would dilute, water down the feeling I had.

You know, I'm basically a jerk when it comes to the finer emotions in life. It was pitiful but I was afraid of confronting myself with my own feelings. Especially because I knew it didn't make much sense. I mean, not if you believe love is about sharing things in common, believing the same things, doing the same stuff. Etain and I didn't have any of that.

Me, I think if love exists at all it's this kind of automatic "click" that you can't control, that doesn't maybe make any sense at all, that you can't rationalize or defend. That's what I believe to the extent that I've ever spent any time thinking about it. Which I never had, until this very night.

So, anyway, I was already awake when the yelling and the running started.

I jumped up, jammed my feet in my skanky old sneaks, and was reasonably clothed when someone started pounding on the door.

"Who is it?" I yelled. Hey, you don't open doors in Everworld without knowing who's on the other side. Or back home, either, for that matter.

"Etain," came the answer and for about a millisecond I tried to resolve the yelling and pounding with the possibility that Etain had dropped by to ask for my hand in marriage and a test drive on the honeymoon. But no, that was pretty unlikely.

I opened the door. She was wearing a robe, full-length but not entirely opaque, mostly covered over by a heavy velvet cloak. Two tough-looking fairies were holding torches that hissed as they burned.

"What's up?" I asked.

"Lorg is dead."

"The giant? What happened?"

"We don't know," she said, and for a moment there was definite suspicion on her part, definite fish-eye. "He was killed by some magic we do not comprehend. We feared . . . we hoped . . . will you come to see his body?"

"Yeah, of course."

The others were being roused out of their

rooms. April and David were in the hallway, having been awakened by fairy soldiers. I was the one Etain had come to waken personally.

Well, all right.

We hustled down dark stone corridors and out into a courtyard where horses were being saddled for us. It was chilly out, and steam came from the horses' nostrils. Their hooves made a lot of noise on cobblestones and an upper window creaked open to reveal the king himself.

Everyone paused in what they were doing to look up at him. You'd expect an old man like him, an old man who'd drunk by my count three bottles of wine to be a bit on the frowzy, confused, hazy side.

No. The old boy was wide-awake. Not pissed exactly, but not happy, either. Taking care of business.

"Daughter," he called down. "Take care to learn the truth. No matter the consequences, learn the truth: I rely upon you."

"Yes, Father."

And then, the weirdest thing. The old man hauled a sheathed sword up from out of sight, and threw it down to Etain. It spun in the air as it fell, and the sword itself came out of the scabbard and I had no time to react, no time to do the hero thing and throw myself in the path of the blade.

Just as well. Etain caught the scabbard with her left hand, and caught the spinning sword with her right hand. And maybe it was just a trick of moonlight, but I swear the blade glowed blue when she touched it.

One of the fairies snapped the scabbard around her waist, under her cloak, and Etain slid that blade in with the practiced ease of Wyatt Earp holstering his six-gun.

She swung up into the saddle of a big, black, snorting monster of a horse and held it in check, prancing, while David and April and Jalil and I all saddled up.

Senna stood alone. They hadn't brought her a horse. Which was a message in itself. Horses won't carry a witch, and the fact that there was no horse for her meant as plain as day that Etain and her family knew perfectly well what Senna was.

"You guys have a broom for Senna?" I asked.

Senna took it all pretty well; no one ever accused her of being a wimp. She didn't say anything, just waited, head high, gray eyes indifferent, above it all. And sure enough, a fairy drove up in a sort of chariot and with studied insolence invited her aboard.

And off we went into the night, out the gate, across the drawbridge, pelting down through a cold fog that had eaten the town and seemed to force refrigerator hands inside my clothes. The moon was up and it wasn't dead dark, but still the countryside beyond the village looked a lot more Tim Burton than it did during the day.

We rode back the way we'd walked earlier, along the road and the incongruous telegraph line. And after a while I could see lights, torches ahead, burning eerily through the mist. We turned off the path to reach the torches.

Lorg was laid out there, splayed on his back, with one leg stuck into a tree and his head in the stream. A platoon of fairies was on guard, holding the whispering torches that cast lurid orange shadows everywhere.

Flat on his back, Lorg seemed as big as ever but strangely vulnerable. It was embarrassing, like walking in on someone in the bathroom. He was so nearly comical, laid out that way, with his big, Toxic Avenger face relaxed into its default expression.

We climbed down off our horses, and Etain went straight to the giant and laid her hand on his sequoia of an arm.

The head fairy reported, "His throat is not cut, my lady. Nor is he dismembered: All his limbs are in place."

Etain didn't want to hear details right then; she

had her eyes closed and I guess was remembering or honoring the big guy. A sort of druid prayer maybe. April made the sign of the cross and seemed to be mumbling her own prayer. When Etain opened her eyes she went first to April and took her hand and squeezed it in thanks. I felt like a jerk having done nothing during the interval but stare, but no one told me there was going to be praying.

Now Etain was ready for business.

"Have you found any tracks?" she asked the fairies.

"Those of yourself and of these men," the fairy said, indicating all of us with the term "men." "And one other man's footprints. Perhaps different from these. But no armed party. No cohort of warriors. No other giants."

"No single man could kill Lorg unless he was a warrior to rival Cu Chulainn."

"Can I . . . ?" It was Jalil. "Excuse me for interrupting. Can I get up on top? Up on Lorg, I mean? I think I see something."

Etain looked dubious. She shot a questioning look at me. I nodded and said, "Maybe you should let him take a look."

I got a slight "give me a break" eye roll from Jalil over that. And I think David was annoyed at the idea I was suddenly Etain's confidant.

Jalil tried climbing up the dead giant's side but it wasn't easy. I gave him a boost and then Jalil gave me a pull and I had the flesh-creeping sensation of walking over yielding, still-warm, but definitely dead flesh.

Jalil led the way from the giant's chest. He balanced on the loose, saggy skin of his massive neck, and peered closely at the right side of Lorg's head.

"We need a torch," Jalil said, and a fairy leaped up to join us.

"Hold it close."

Jalil pointed. Holes that seemed absurdly small, tiny wormholes in under the hairline. A dozen or fifteen holes in a random pattern. And another similar pattern of holes above one misshapen eye.

Jalil took a deep breath and gave me a covert look. "Am I crazy?" he asked in a whisper.

I shook my head. "No. I mean, I've never seen any in real life, but you know, on TV and all."

"What is it?" David demanded.

Jalil said, "Etain, I'd suggest you have your people scour the area, for about a hundred yards in every direction. Have them look for small cylinders made of brass." He held up his fingers to show the size.

"What the —" David began, then he got it. "There's no way, Jalil."

The fairies didn't take long. "Here, my lady," one of them called out from a spot maybe fifty feet downstream. The fairy came zooming back. His hand was full of clinking brass cylinders, half an inch long.

Jalil started to climb down, anxious to play the part of Sherlock Holmes, I guess. I was coming down right behind him when I happened to look over and see Senna. I was looking at her as Jalil said the words, "Automatic weapon. Some kind of machine gun. Someone shot the guy. Someone shot the hell out of him."

CHAPTER VIII

The sun came up watery and mist-filtered on a far busier scene. Old Lorg was still dead. But now the king had come with the type of guys we'd met in passing a long time before and a long way away: Fianna.

The Fianna, as I understood it, were knights of a sort, though they didn't go in for the whole shining-armor thing. They were the personal army of the High King. I figured the High King was like the president, with King Camulos being a governor. King Cam's fairies were the state troopers, the Fianna were the FBI and the marines all rolled into one.

The Fiannans were quiet and polite and respectful. They addressed everyone by their title, or else as "sir" or "lady." They'd ridden through the night in response to a telegram sent by the king and arrived from the distant capital. Their massive horses were wandering around the fields eating grass.

A bunch of druids had also showed up. We had blue druids and green druids and red druids. It was a druid convention, but not what a person might picture: They were old and young, male and female, snappy dressers or old slobs. The one thing they all seemed to have in common was an incredible lack of stupidity.

The blue druids spent quite a while going over the giant's already fragrant body, poking, probing, and finally cutting. There was some discussion of dissecting Lorg — dissection was all the rage with blue druids — but no one had invented the chain saw yet, so it was hard to see how they were going to carve him up.

Still, they used handy scalpels and lancets and clunky, ornate tweezers, and pretty soon they had removed his canned ham of an eye and collected half a dozen bullets.

Jalil was busy being cross-examined by Fios, the only yellow druid there. I was hearing words like "firing pin" and "barrel" and "magazine." Fios was nodding like a psychiatrist who has just heard your sickest fantasy but doesn't want to act too grossed-out. Jalil looked embarrassed.

One of the blue druids, a chubby, grandmotherly woman, came over to me carrying a pottery jar with six bloody lumps rolling around inside.

"What are these called?" she asked me.

"Those are slugs. They're made of lead. Mostly, anyway. I guess there's copper, too. The copper holds them together a little, but see, the head of the slug still spreads out, mashes up, when it hits."

Grandma Druid gave me a funny look. "How does lead come to flatten thus? Even lead, softest of metals, is harder than flesh."

"Well, it's going very fast. Faster than an arrow. I mean, a lot faster. It hits and . . . *wham*. The lead flattens and then it tears through the muscle or whatever and . . ." I was performing helpful hand gestures to illustrate.

You know, I'd have been happy to explain bullets to Ka Anor. Or Loki. Or Hel. Or Neptune. I'd have been happy to explain bullets in the most direct, hands-on way I could, but having to stand there and explain how a bullet tore through flesh and muscle and organs, explain all that to these decent-seeming people, that wasn't easy. Hard not to feel responsible.

"Ah," she said, and rolled the slugs back and forth.

Just then a fairy came zooming in to report to the king. They'd found a small boat floating just offshore. A fishing boat, abandoned. And on the shore, wedged into the rocks, two dead fishermen who bore the same puncture wounds found in Lorg.

David had rounded up Jalil and April and gathered me up and the four of us stepped off a way from the crime-scene crowd.

"Someone's got a machine gun," David said in a low voice.

"Do you think so, McGarrett?" I said. "What gave it away?"

He clenched his jaw and looked like he wanted to hit me and only just restrained himself.

"We're kind of deep in it here," David snapped. "Maybe not the time for sarcasm. None of these people is a fool: They're thinking we're responsible somehow."

Jalil shook his head. "No. We've given the Coo-Hatch some technology to make cannons. But from muzzle-loading cannons to full-auto weapons, that's a couple centuries."

"Senna's behind this," I said suddenly.

David's head snapped up, angry. "Don't say things like that. You want them to hear?"

"You know he's right," April said. "You know it's her. Otherwise why is it the four of us here talking and not Senna? You left her out, David. Why is that?"

I said, "I saw her, I was watching her when Jalil started talking about guns. Not a flicker. She didn't jerk guiltily, but she didn't jerk surprised, either."

The four of us turned slowly and stared at Senna. She stood off by herself, pacing very slowly, looking as if she were taking a slow-motion tour of the stone walls. Deep in thought.

I noticed the head Fiannan, a guy with the excellent name of MacCool. He was watching us and watching our faces as we looked at Senna. It was a "cop" look.

I looked back at Senna. She was gone, hidden by some wafting mist.

MacCool wasn't so sure.

"The witch," he said loudly. "Where is the witch?"

A breeze blew the mist away. No Senna.

Fairies erupted into a blur, racing here and there, fanning out. The Fiannans spread out a bit more slowly than the fairies.

April left us and walked straight to Etain. She grabbed her arm.

David yelled, "April!"

Too late. "She's a shape-shifter," April said. "She could be anyone."

Etain nodded. "MacCool! The witch can change shape." Etain came striding over to us, suspicious, furious at everyone except April. "You should have warned me."

"She's one of us," David shot back.

"The hell she is." Jalil.

"We came here together!" David yelled, suddenly almost out of control. "We came here together, we leave together, all of us, her, too!"

I said, "We didn't come here, General, we were dragged. By her." To Etain I said, "We lied to you last night. We're here because Senna dragged us here. She's some kind of gateway between the old world and Everworld and she's also a freaking nut. She's got a power jones. She wants to be the newer, better Ka Anor. We've been her little sock puppets all along."

April joined in. "She's completely ruthless. And she has powers. More power all the time." She looked right at David. "Don't let her touch any of your people, Etain. That's how she's strongest."

"Why not just tell them to shoot on sight?" David demanded.

I said, "David, she's an evil bitch who sells us out anytime it suits her. We're supposed to be loyal? To her?"

"We stick together!" David almost screamed. "I know it looks bad. I know . . . but we stick together, man, that's the thing."

Jalil stepped close to David, got right in his

face. "David, there's someone over here running around with a damned Uzi. And we all know somehow she's behind it."

Then suddenly Jalil grabbed David's arms, not like he was trying to control him, more like he was trying to hold himself up. Like someone had sucked the air out of his lungs and he needed to hold on or faint.

"What is it?" April asked.

"That's what she's going to do," Jalil said in a whisper. "That's what she's going to do. A gateway goes both ways. Of course. Oh, Jesus."

"Shut up, Jalil," David said, but there was no conviction behind it.

Jalil looked horrified, stared at David. "You guessed! You knew?"

David was wringing his hands, saying, "Just shut up, Jalil." As messed up as I have ever seen David. He looked like someone was piling bricks on his shoulders, like some growing weight was crushing him slowly down.

"David, you poor dumb son of a —"

I lost patience at the same moment as April. "What?" we both yelled. "What?"

Jalil wiped his face with his hand, wiped off the sweat and the fog condensation. "You open a door between universes, who's to say which way the traffic flows?"

"Did you find that in a fortune cookie?"

"Senna won't let anyone use her. She wants power. She's not going to be Loki's tool, or anyone's tool. She's the gateway, she knows that. But it's not about whether she's going to let Loki and the others escape into the real world. The traffic's going the other way, man. She's bringing people here. She's bringing them here. Men with guns."

It was a moment of crystalline revelation. It took my breath away. I laughed. Of course!

Senna was in a bind: If Merlin caught her she'd be locked away in his tower forever. If Loki caught her she'd be forced to become his gateway, open an escape route to the real world.

Neither choice exactly worked for Senna. Senna wanted it all. She knew her own magic was nowhere near powerful enough to make her a player in Everworld. Ah, but Senna with an army, an army with real-world weapons, that was a different story.

Lorg the giant was dead. The perfect symbol: Everworld's Goliath versus a real-world David carrying an Uzi slingshot. Bye-bye, Goliath.

CHAPTER IX

We horsed up and headed back eventually to the town and King Cam's castle. All of us together, leaving behind some of the Fianna and a number of fairies. But MacCool rode with us. Rode right next to Etain as a matter of fact. Right alongside her.

And that really should not have been tippy-top of my brain right then, what with all that had happened, what with the fact that Senna had escaped, but the brain and the body do what they want to do. Especially when the brain gets together with the body.

It's like the body is the bad friend your mom doesn't want you to hang around with, because, man, however good your brain wants to be, however many promises old brainiac makes, body can always bring him over to the dark side of the force.

Body was having a Harlequin kind of morning. Brain was trying real hard to be serious and focus on the fact that good old Senna had come up and kicked the chessboard all over the place so that all of a sudden no one could remember where the pieces had been before. But body was mainlining testosterone and looking to find some friendly estrogen. The Y chromosome wanted to go say hi to the double X's. Body had its own separate memory of Etain's nightgown. And body had been strangely excited by Etain's cool sword trick. Brain never had a chance.

And the thing was that MacCool was putting the moves on Etain. Not that she'd notice, naturally: Girls are always prepared to believe that a guy has something else in mind. Despite roughly a million years of human experience, females persist in their belief that deep down inside, guys are girls.

No doubt MacCool was talking about the killing. No doubt he was very professional. He looked like that kind of guy. But he was a hound, I had no doubt. He was giving her the thoughtful look, the considering nod, the old leaning-close-to-hear-better-while-inspecting-cleavage move.

I decided to demonstrate my maturity by pouting. Fine. Forget her. There were plenty more beautiful half-elf maidens who would jump at the chance to hook up with a penniless, cowardly minstrel from another universe.

My horse wasn't fast and I wasn't interested in pushing him. So my horse moseyed and stopped to munch, and I moseyed and pouted and wondered whether it really was just coincidence that Etain had come personally to my room.

I was at the back of the column, back behind the afterguard of Fianna and fairies. Just me and some sleepy, yawning, uniformed guy from the palace, and one of the Fianna, one of MacCool's boys leading a lame horse.

We came to a curve in the path as it went around a stand of trees, the three of us were bringing up the rear, and temporarily blocked from the view of the king and MacCool and Etain and David and the rest of the Important People.

The Fiannan decided to give up on keeping pace with his lame horse. He sighed and yanked his horse around and started back down the road from the direction we'd come. Taking the lame horse back to . . .

Back to what? Why not lead the horse on to the village?

I looked back just before I'd have lost sight of him entirely. And that's when I saw him abandon his horse and climb over a stone fence.

I knew right away. I knew it cold: It was Senna.

What I should do is race up the path, alert the
king, who'd send MacCool pelting back after her.
And if MacCool or the fairies caught her I'd get a
nice pat on the head.

I could see that scene, clear as day: MacCool
with a sullen Senna in tow, me trotting along
yelping, "I saw her! I saw her! I'm the one who
saw her!"

Yeah. That would have Etain throwing Mac-
Cool aside in favor of me. 'Cause if there's one
thing a woman admires, it's a guy who can call
for the help of a real man.

I reined in my horse. The sleepy uniformed guy
kept going, and I thought for a second of telling
him what I was doing, but no, he'd just go grab
MacCool.

Screw MacCool.

I turned my horse. I could do this. I had a
horse, Senna was on foot. Besides, I knew she'd be
tired. We knew that about her, that doing the
magic thing wore her out. She must have been
shape-shifting for half an hour at least, and she'd
be beat. Sometimes the tiredness put her under,
unconscious.

"Come on, Christopher. You're not scared of
Senna," I told myself. But here's the thing: Any
time you have to deny that you're scared, you're
scared.

"It's just Senna," I told myself. "It's not like she's a troll, or a god, or something really nasty."

No, it was just good old Senna. I had dated her. I'd kissed her. Of course, that was before I'd seen her literally shift the course of an entire river.

"Man, you're meat," I told myself.

I couldn't see Senna anymore. There were widely spaced trees and a slight up-slope. Maybe she was back in the trees. Maybe she was over the rise. Maybe she was asleep. Maybe she was gone altogether.

I had no weapon. But now I was in it, I couldn't wimp out. So I urged my horse to jump the stone fence. He didn't exactly jump. More like stumbled. We kicked over some rocks and the horse complained, although not in English, which was a relief.

I urged my horse onward and began searching desperately for a big stick, anything I could use as a weapon. I told myself that if I screamed the fairies would be all over us in a few seconds, but I didn't believe it. The fairies were fast but they weren't everywhere at once. And by now the king and Etain and my friends were all ten minutes farther down the path. Didn't they even notice I wasn't there? I mean, if they all came riding back after me and arrived just as I found Senna, hey, I'd get full credit for being brave and for catching the witch. I'd be content with that. I'd have the intention of bravery — that was as good as actual bravery.

I topped the rise, leaning forward over the horse's neck to stay on in the slope. On the other side was a dell, I guess that's what you'd call it. A sort of shallow dimple in the land, maybe a hundred feet across, grassy in most places, more sparse under the gloomy trees.

In the center of the dell was a circle of crudely cut stone pillars the size of upended Land Cruisers. Twelve in all, and each topped with a precariously balanced stone about big enough to eat dinner off of.

There in the center of the circle, shining through the mist, stood Senna.

I felt a chill go right through me. It was damp, and it was cold, and I was tired, but none of that was the reason for the chill.

She was very calm, waiting, not exactly relaxed, but not ready to go Jackie Chan on me, either. I reined in well outside the circle of stones.

"Druid stones, like Stonehenge," Senna said
conversationally, like I'd asked her a question.
"They seem to have advanced quite a way since
the days when they used these kinds of circles to
plot the stars and the moon and regulate the
planting days and the holidays and the harvests."

"Yeah," I said, dry-mouthed. "They have cal-
endars now, I guess. Probably those Tolkien cal-
endars. You know . . . like . . . okay."

"What am I supposed to do with you, Christopher?" Senna asked, cocking her head to one side.

"Come back with me," I said as firmly as I
could.

She smiled and shook her head regretfully. "I

don't think so, Christopher. These folks are simple, but not stupid. They know that what happened to Lorg wasn't magic. They know we're involved in some way. And you or Jalil or April would have sold me out to them."

I could deny it, but what would be the point? "Yeah. Not me, though. Not that I wouldn't, it's just that I would never have had a chance: It would be a toss-up between Jalil and April. Me, I don't like you, don't trust you, but I don't have a major beef with you."

She nodded, accepting that. "I wish I could trust you, Christopher, I really do."

"Can I kill him now?" a voice asked.

That voice . . . familiar. From somewhere, not here, but from somewhere. I looked around, saw no one. Just the stones, the trees, the grass.

"Yes, you can kill him now."

Keith loomed up from atop one of the massive rocks, rising to his full, not-very-impressive height. He cradled an Uzi in the crook of one arm. There was a pair of pistols holstered around his waist. An ammo belt hung over one shoulder.

Keith, the sick little racist Nazi wanna-be punk who had threatened me over in the real world. I didn't pause to wonder how in hell he'd ended up here now, I just moved. Kicked my horse hard with both heels and rolled backward off him. Bang onto my back, thank God for soft grass, and still the wind was kicked out of me.

The Uzi erupted and the horse screamed. The horse hit the ground, kicked, then stopped kicking.

I rolled up against the base of the nearest stone pillar. Tried to think. Keith. With a freaking Uzi. A little Klebold-Harris psychopath working with Senna. And me with nothing but handfuls of grass.

I heard Keith above. He was leaping from stone table to stone table. Leaping heavily. He was weighed down with all that hardware, not like me, no, boy, thank goodness I had nothing to contend with but empty freaking hands. If I ran for the trees he'd have a perfect, easy shot at me. If I stayed in the stones he'd have a harder time, but there was Senna to deal with.

All I had survived in Everworld and I was going to get shot? Shot? With a gun?

I breathed hard, almost sobbing. How did David do this hero crap? What should I do? Slight vibration down through the stone pillar. Keith was directly above me. So at least he was no genius: How was he going to shoot me when he couldn't lean out far enough to see me?

Loud explosions all around me, clattering, chipping, exploding rock.

I scampered around the rock. Keith was sticking his gun over the edge and firing blind and had damned near greased me. I crawled fast, elbows on grass, thinking, *The stains will never come out*, thinking it was almost funny, and when I came full circle there would be Senna and I'd be all done.

A blur that came to a sudden vibrating stop. Two fairies at the top of the rise. They stared hard.

"Run!" I yelled. "Get help, run!"

A stream of bullets caught them, spun one around. He was dead before he hit the grass. The other ran, but he was hit. Too badly to get away? Couldn't tell, couldn't see.

I scurried around the rock and there was Senna. But she wasn't looking at me. She wasn't looking at anything. She was glowing like she'd swallowed a stadium light. Her head was thrown back, her arms spread wide in a parody of crucifixion, eyes staring up at nothing.

The light inside her shined right through her, she was translucent, insubstantial. She was hard to look at, she was so bright.

Keith was capering away atop his rock yelling, "Yee-hah! Yeah! Yeah!" and other hillbilly nitwit witticisms. "Now it comes! Now it comes down! It's happening right now!"

And then he remembered his business and aimed a blast at where I'd been a few seconds before. I rolled over to look up and see if I could spot the muzzle before he could kill me.

Help had to be on the way, right? Come on, MacCool, come on, David, someone save my sorry ass.

The air around Senna was shimmering, a wind had whipped up, a wind that seemed to blow straight through her, like she was an open window in a gale.

The gateway! She was doing it. She was opening the gateway.

"Yeah! Yeah! Do it! King of the world!" Keith yammered.

And then, as I blinked in disbelief, I was looking right through Senna, right through her at a shabby room, a real-world room. Maybe a dozen men, maybe twice that many, were somehow inside her. Men of various ages, all of them gaping in some mixture of terror and weird exaltation.

All of them were armed, most with more than one weapon. They had dark green ammo boxes piled up around their ankles. One was wearing a swastika armband.

Keith yelled and just fired into the air in celebration. It came to me then that it was right now or never. Right this minute or I was never getting out of this place.

I jumped up and ran from my rock to the next rock over, expecting the line of bullets to shatter my spine. I raced around the far side and hugged rock, weeping. I hugged that damp rock, held on, didn't want to let go.

"Keep going," I told myself and damned if I didn't. I ran to the next rock. Now I'd be blocked from Keith's view, at least for a while. If I ran straight for the trees, quick calculation, he'd see me, oh yes he'd see me, but how much exposed space did I have to cover? He'd blown away the fairies at an even longer distance.

No choice, moron, run!

I ran. Ran for the trees, bounding along over the springy grass, with the sound of a tornado growing behind me, punctuated by Keith's mad ranting.

Then . . .

A loud curse. *BamBamBam.* I jerked with each explosion. Saw the line of bullets hit the grass beside me, move toward me, no way to outrun it, the advancing line of bullets . . . stopped! Empty clip.

Another curse, frantic now.

I was still running, still laboring up the slope

when he opened up with his pistols. Two shots. Then I was in the trees, slid behind the first like Daffy Duck with Elmer Fudd on his tail.

Bullets thudded into the tree. The far side of the tree. I ran again, this time keeping the tree between me and Keith and now the range was too far for accuracy. The shots were wild and I was out of the dell, over the lip of the ridge, and running like I was trying out for the fairy Olympics.

"At least a dozen. Maybe more. Lots of guns. A whole Keanu-load of guns. Boxes of ammunition. I don't know what all else."

I was back in the castle, back behind walls that didn't seem nearly high enough or thick enough anymore. Etain, the king, Queen Goewynne, Mac-Cool, Fios, and a representative from each color of druid, plus all my friends, were there.

Everyone was scared. Or at least everyone who got it was scared. Some of them were not understanding the deal, despite the testimony of the second fairy, the one who had taken a slug in his scrawny butt but still managed to limp home.

"At least a dozen heavily armed electroshock cases. I mean, Jalil and I know Keith, all right? If he's an example of these guys, we're talking major meltdowns, whack jobs: cousin-marrying, beer-for-breakfast, swastika-tattooed losers who stay up all night stroking their guns and watching *Saving Private Ryan* so they can root for the Germans."

"Only twelve?" MacCool said with the slightest little smile of condescension. "Twelve mortals?"

"No," I said, pounding the table with the reckless rudeness of a man who'd just finally stopped shaking, "Twelve guys with subma-freaking-chine guns, all right? See everyone in this room? Here's how long it takes." I stood up and pointed my finger like a gun. "*BamBamBamBamBamBam*, you're all dead, all right? Keith killed the two fishermen. He killed your big old giant, all right? He smoked one of your fairies and almost got the other one."

David said, "He's right. The fairies are so fast and so accurate with their bows that you folks could probably put up a good fight, especially if this little army is as disorganized and untrained as I suspect they are. But I'll tell you flat out: if the twelve of them are under the control of someone smart and organized and patient . . ."

"Senna," April said poisonously.

David flinched. I wanted to feel sorry for him. He'd been bewitched by Senna — and in Everworld that's not just a cliché. But to some extent his continued devotion to Senna was his own choice. Plus he had it in his head that he was the brave platoon leader who was going to get us all out safely, come hell or high water. It's no joke being trapped in those macho fantasies, you know: doesn't leave you much room for being a normal human being.

"The question is where she gets these people," Jalil said thoughtfully. "I mean, how do you recruit heavily armed nuts?"

"NRA convention?" April cracked.

"She's recruiting these guys on the other side, in the real world," Jalil said. "Guys who'll give up home and family and job for what?"

"Adventure," I supplied. "The chance to swagger and point a gun and have people kiss their butts. Why do you think people do anything? They want power. You should have heard Keith up there, dancing around and 'yee-hahing.' I mean, he's a nobody. He's a loser. It's not exactly some software billionaire or boy genius who is going to join up with this kind of stuff."

I guess MacCool felt like things were getting away from him, so he stood up, drawing every eye. "The Fianna have protected this land and kept the peace for generations. We have protected our shores from Vikings and Saxons, our skies from dragons and griffins, our forests from demons and goblins. No Hetwan has walked Eire's sacred soil and lived. We will meet this new challenge. I assure you of that."

The king's eyes lit up. He slapped the table. "Well said. Hear him."

Etain's eyes lit up, too. "I will go with you. I put my faith in the Fianna."

Oh, man. Great. Unbelievable. She was falling for that act? She'd get herself killed. That posturing tough guy MacCool would get her killed.

I was startled to discover Goewynne staring right at me. It was a laser of a stare. She'd seen my petulant eye rolling. But she'd seen my worry, too, I guess. With the slightest turn of her head she sent me a silent question. I met her gaze and shook my head slowly, emphatically: *No, lady, you don't let Etain go or she comes back dead.*

"No, daughter, you must stay with us. We require your help and sage counsel," Goewynne said.

"I'll go with you," David said heavily.

"I would welcome Galahad's sword," MacCool boomed expansively. Good grief, he was more David than David, and that's way too much David.

I swear I half expected the two nitwit heroes to start high-fiving each other. But David ain't stupid. I mean, he's dumb, but not downright stupid.

But instead David just snorted, almost contemptuously. "Galahad's sword? Up against machine guns? MacCool, I'm not going along because I think you'll succeed. I'm going because maybe I can try to influence Senna. And maybe I can help save some of your people. You people go up against these guys waving swords, you'll die. At least bring fairy archers along, a lot of them."

MacCool's cool MacCool eyes flashed. "The Fianna honor the fairy bowmen, but the Fianna fight alone."

"I'll go with you," I said, startling myself and earning an honest surprised look from Elf Mommy, and a look of warm appreciation from Etain.

"You will?" April said, more puzzled than impressed.

"Yeah. Someone's going to need to show these two heroes how to run away."

CHAPTER

XII

Jalil and April stayed behind. They'd both volunteered to come along, falling in with the general mood of suicidal stupidity that had overcome all of us.

But David pulled Jalil aside and begged him not to. "We're going to get our asses kicked, and we're going to come running back here. Someone needs to get these people to prepare, or Senna's army will just roll right in. The fairy archers are the only hope: They're fast, they're accurate. Get to the captain of the fairies and talk to him: Explain about guns. Don't take any b.s. And if they have some magic thing they can do, don't bitch them out about it, okay? Just for once, go with the magic."

Jalil agreed. And then David, looking guilty and worried, talked to April. "There's something

Jalil knows, but the rest of you don't: One of their gods is over in the real world. One of the Celtic gods, I mean, a goddess named Brigid. She lives up on Sheridan."

"Say what?" I said.

"It's a long story." He told April the address.

"Yeah, well, take five minutes and explain how you know that a goddess just happens to be living on the lake?"

David ignored me and focused on April. "Go to sleep, if you can, cross over, and go see this woman, this Brigid. Don't let her blow you off. Sometimes she passes herself off as a maid. Tell her what's happening over here. I don't know what her powers are, but tell her. Maybe she can . . . I don't what she can do."

April was obviously torn. She's not one to hide when the trouble starts. But she could see the logic of what David proposed. "Anyway," she muttered, "maybe I'll be there for my own performance. *Rent* is tonight. Or yesterday — who knows with the weird time thing."

"This is messed up," I said. The whole thing had the feeling of a final farewell. David was worried and so was I. But then, worry is my life, so that was okay. On balance it's probably better to get shot than to be chewed up by a giant. Not that either was a good idea.

"You can stay here in the castle, help Jalil," David said to me.

I gave David a respectful salute involving a raised middle finger.

MacCool had twenty guys with him. They did look like a fairly tough crew. There were few unscarred faces. There were a number of missing fingers and ears and even one nose. They all had that calm, cool, combat-veteran nonchalance. They checked their weapons and their saddles and made sure their water bottles were topped off — although it's just possible the bottles contained something a bit rougher than water. I wished mine did.

David and I were given horses and I was provided with a sword.

"All I need to do is learn that Wonder Woman thing where she blocks the bullets real fast with her magic bracelets," I said, trying the sword's weight in my hand.

"Stay toward the back," David said in an undertone.

"I'll ride with you," I said boldly. "I can be just as big a jackass as you, David."

Once we were all saddled up, the king and queen and Etain and a crowd of well-wishers came to see us off. There were brave words and

exhortations. And then Goewynne and Etain unwound scarves from around their necks. I groaned
inwardly. I knew this scene: The hot medieval
babe ties her scarf around the neck or shoulder
or — if they're totally pre-Freudian — lance, of
her hero.

Goewynne went up to MacCool and said some
well-chosen words and tied her colors around the
big goof's neck. I almost laughed. Was MacCool
getting nasty with Mom? No, no, her husband
the king was applauding the gesture.

Then again, maybe old Camulos was playing
Arthur to Mac's Lancelot. I considered a joke involving "a lot of lancing" and decided against it
on the grounds that no one would laugh, and besides, I felt like throwing up.

I was busy mulling all this when Etain cleared
her throat impatiently to get my attention. And
damned if she wasn't standing there with her
scarf all loaded up for me. I almost fell off the
horse lowering my head to receive the honor.

"Thanks," I said with terrific eloquence.

"I thought it might give you courage," she said,
grinning with the kind of perfect teeth that are
more rare in Everworld than cell phones.

"It'll take more than that," I said. And what
was cool, what was so perfectly cool, was that she

laughed along with me and we looked at each other and there was this moment, this true moment.

One of the druids came and chanted some stuff, a sort of blessing, I guess — I was focusing on Etain. And then, at a jaunty command from MacCool we rode off, "Hi-yo, Silver," clattering out through the castle gate, rumbling across the drawbridge, down the steeply down-sloping cobblestone street, past cheering, waving, admiring town peasants, all of whom were thinking, *Better them than me.*

Off we went at a nice gallop, David and me just behind MacCool and his number-two man, a skinny, gray-bearded, mean-looking old guy named Fraich who could only count to seven on his fingers, and to one on his ears.

We passed the cable car, running empty but for its crew. The two liveried hangers-on, footmen, I guess, gave us a bow.

Just as we reached the far edge of town MacCool broke out of the column to review us as we passed and to pull off a neat little trick: He whipped his sword up out of its scabbard, threw it twirling end over end way up in the air, and caught it by the pommel just as the point was about to plunge into his area. The suckers loved it. Big huge cheer and cries of encouragement from the onlookers.

Still and all, it did prove that MacCool could handle a sword. Almost as well as Etain had done the night before. Maybe she should have come along.

"You're jealous, aren't you?" I said to David. "Wish you could do that, don't you?"

A rare David smile. "Damn right."

We trotted along the road out of town, out into the stone-fence-and-clumps-of-moss countryside. It was maybe two miles to the stone circle where Senna had opened herself up as the gateway. Between here and there the road followed the stream mostly. At places the road was shadowed by clumps of trees, or edged by tumbles of scabbed green-and-white boulders.

"What will she do?" I wondered aloud.

"Senna?" David sighed in that deep, depressed way he had whenever Senna was the topic. "She knows we're on to her. She knows we're going to try to counter her advantage. Given enough time we could neutralize it. If we reached the Coo-Hatch and shared all we know, they . . ." He fell silent.

"Yeah," I said. "We arranged for the Coo-Hatch to bail out of Everworld, didn't we? With Senna's help. No way to know how many Coo-Hatch have made it back to their own real world, but one way or the other, there are going to be fewer of them. You've been outgeneraled, General. Senna let us force her into removing the one bunch of people in this nuthouse who could have built guns for us."

He had nothing to say for a long time as we rode in morose silence, filled with the sphincter-tightening expectation that we were in someone's sights.

Finally he said, "It would be a mistake to overestimate her. She's not ten feet tall. She knows guns are useful, doesn't mean she knows how to use them."

"We got swords, she's got machine guns," I said.

"She's going to ambush us," David said with certainty. "She doesn't count me for much, obviously, but she's scared of Jalil. She's going to try to go for a fast kill. Hit us hard, take the castle, kill all of us. She's not ten feet tall but she's smart: Her edge is technology. She knows that Jalil can eventually wipe out that edge. She's seen how quick these folks are to adopt modern technology, telegraph lines going up, that cable car, primitive electricity."

"You reading her mind now?" I said. "Kind of late, isn't it, Maximus?"

"Yeah, it is kind of late," he said. He spurred his horse a bit and caught up with MacCool. "Listen, MacCool, I'm going to tell you what's going to happen. You can believe me or not, but when it happens you need to remember what I'm telling you."

MacCool gave him the condescending up-and-down look the serious hero reserves for the wanna-be. But he let David talk just the same.

"One of these little clumps of trees, like this very one we're riding into, they'll be waiting. They'll be on both sides of the road, concealed, you won't see them. Then all of a sudden it's going to be like a lightning storm: A lot of very loud noise and bright flashes, and your men and horses are going to start dying. But not all of them. The ones who aren't dead right away need to get down off their horses and run away, staying as low to the ground as they can."

"Run away!" MacCool yelled. "Run away, is it? And run away crouching low like beaten dogs, no less?"

"Yes, that's exactly right," David said.

"Listen, stranger, the Fianna do not run."

"I figured you'd say that, MacCool. But I had to

try. Now my friend and I are going to drop back to the tail of this column. And when it happens I'll try my best to get some of your men out of here alive."

David turned his horse and rode to the rear with me following. I don't believe I've ever liked David more than at that moment.

"Ride all the way back to the village and find yourselves a good root cellar in which to cower!" MacCool jeered at our backs. "We need no —"

The burst blew a hole in his chest and knocked him off his horse. His horse died at the same time.

XIII

Flashes from the stone fence to our right. Flashes and yells from the trees on our left. A sudden, deafening clatter all around.

Fraich had time to yell, "Charge!" before a round hit his outstretched right arm. The man nearest to him slumped in his saddle and fell over.

"Dismount!" David yelled.

"Charge!"

Two more men fell. Horses, too. Some were trying to organize for a charge but they were dying before they could spur forward.

"Dismount, damn it!" David yelled, and swung himself down just as his horse's head jerked sideways and an exit hole appeared beneath the animal's eye.

I rolled off, hit the ground, got up into a

crouch, and scampered toward the rear. I heard the mad-bee zing of bullets passing just over my head.

"Get off your horses, you idiots!" David roared. "Get down! Get down!"

Most of the Fianna were still ignoring him, but I guess the logic of the situation was looking pretty convincing to others. Men were climbing down off horses. Those that insisted on sitting high and proud were being ripped apart.

And yet, three of them managed to spur their horses forward and charge straight at the fence. It was glorious, it really was. I saw one of Senna's killers rise up into clear view, take aim, and fire. The first horseman fell straight back.

More fire, and men and horses died, still twenty yards from the fence.

"Down, down, use the horses for cover," David was shouting. And all at once, David was boss. Men were listening. I saw scared tough guys crouching behind dead horses. I saw others crouch-walking like me, bailing out, heading for home. Fraich was one of them. He was dragging his useless right arm, trailing blood.

"Grab those horses," David instructed. "Grab the reins, lead them, keep them between you and the enemy."

We backed away as fast as we could move, lead-

ing the kicking, rearing, scare-masked horses behind us as shields. They died and fell, but we only
had to get over a slight rise in the path to be out
of the line of fire. Fifty feet maybe. Already the
fire was becoming less accurate and intense. The
killers were yelling triumphantly, like sports fans
smelling victory.

I ran, the others ran, we all ran, no horses left
for cover, ran and topped the slight rise and ran
all the faster. But then, just ahead, right across the
road was a stone fence that had definitely not
been there ten minutes earlier. A stone fence
that was building itself higher and higher, like
an army of invisible stonemasons were working.
Stones flew through the air, flew like iron filings
going to a magnet, zoomed through the air from
the surrounding fences.

The fence was rising fast and behind us I heard
a familiar voice crying, "Go after them! Finish
them off!"

I'll tell you something: Lots of guys have sto-
ries about ex-girlfriends from hell, but I was
pretty sure I had a special case.

A whirlwind of head-sized rocks ahead, an advancing wave of flying lead behind. Another Fiannan caught a bullet in the back, stood up,
arched all the way back like he was trying to do a
backflip, and collapsed.

We were screwed, well and truly screwed.

"Get past the fence and we're safe," David yelled.

"What?"

"Cover your head with your hands and arms, run for it!" he said. Then he demonstrated and followed his own advice. A flying rock nailed him in the side. Another caught him in the side of the head and spun him around. He plowed into the rising fence, now nearly six feet tall, scrambled up the side, slammed again in the kidneys.

I was right behind him, arms twisted all around my head, crouching, running, staggering when the rock hit me right between the shoulder blades. Up and running again, cover your head!

Wham. I was down, head swimming, sky and clouds spinning around and around, some guy leaped over me, rocks flying like big demented crows. I rolled over and started crawling the wrong way. Turned again, staggered up, ran, was nailed in the butt by a rock. And now the rocks in the fence were being chipped and hammered by bullets.

Into the wall, legs climbing, kicking, scrabbling, one hand grabbing, the other trying to cover my head, and *bang* something hit me in the face. But I was off the ground, climbing, all at once falling, rolling over onto the far side of the fence.

David was there, face bloody. He grabbed me by the arm and yanked me to my feet. I couldn't see out of my left eye. Something hurt. Everything hurt. Me and David and half a dozen Fianna ran exactly like beaten dogs, tails between our legs, scared to death, bruised and bloody.

Of the twenty-three men and horses who had ridden away from the castle an hour earlier, nine men came dragging back, reaching the gates just as the sun declined past noon.

We rode the fancy cable car the last quarter mile through a town no longer cheering.

CHAPTER
XIV

The town looked nearly abandoned as we lurched along. Windows were shuttered, although you could see eyes peeping out occasionally. A definite change from our happy send-off. News had traveled fast, faster than we ourselves.

"Jalil's been busy," David said approvingly, nodding his blood-caked head.

We reached the castle and slunk through the main gate like the losers we were. Fraich collapsed right away. We had stopped most of the major external bleeding from his arm with jury-rigged pressure bandages. But after a while we'd noticed he had another hole in him, right through the belly.

Once we were in the courtyard they raised the gate and slammed home a big crossbar. I could see that David was right: The castle walls were lined with fairy archers. King Camulos came out to meet us. He was armored up and wearing a big, jeweled sword. He was a different guy now. Not the happy glutton, not even the concerned king. He was mad as hell in a cold-blooded kind of way.

"Where is MacCool?" the king demanded.

"Dead," David said.

"Fraich?"

"Over there. He's alive. But he won't be for long," David reported. "Where is Jalil?"

All the while we were staggering to the keep, the biggest of the towers. Inside, in a vast, echoing room alive with busy soldiers, human and fairy, I felt a little better. Now I had two sets of walls between me and Senna.

Etain came running up, pushing her way past men who were suiting up in useless armor. She made a pained face on seeing me.

"Jeez, do I look that bad?"

"Do you not know?" She touched my brow gently. "The flesh is torn. Hanging loose, here. It will need sewing up."

"Gross," I said.

Jalil came running up. "You guys okay?"

"Yeah, Jalil. We're great. Why do you ask?"

"King Camulos, with every respect, I need to be put in charge of defending this place," David said. "I need your authority to act."

"I command here," the king snapped. Then he looked around at what was left of MacCool's elite troops and he softened. "But I heed my good advisers. I have done all that your friend Jalil has advised me to do."

Jalil nodded. "We have every fairy archer we could find manning the walls. The armorers are turning out arrows as fast as they can. We've got the village locked up tight down below."

"That's good," David said. "Very good. But she expects us to wait here for her. She won the first round. She may get cocky. How about April?" he asked, changing gears suddenly.

"She's trying to sleep," Jalil said. "Not as easy as you might think."

"Okay, sir. King Camulos, here's what I need: a dozen of your best bowmen. Six to go with me, six to go with Christopher."

"I volunteered? Man, I gotta learn to keep my mouth shut."

"You don't want payback?" David asked me.

"No, that's you, not me, David. But I'll do it anyway. You know why?"

"No," he admitted honestly.

"Because you're just so cute when you go all Napoleon."

"You're an idiot," he said, but he laughed as he said it. "Jalil, man, you know what's what here at the castle, stay on this end."

Etain unwound the scarf from around my neck. It was saturated with blood, most of it probably mine, and with fear-sweat, all of it mine.

"I shall replace this," Etain said softly.

"Better wash it. Or maybe burn it," I said apologetically.

"Never," she said. "Blood shed in defense of my land can never offend."

She so totally wanted me. And I so totally wanted a shower and a meal and a case of beer. But after all that I'd have liked nothing better than to cuddle up with Etain somewhere, good lord, she was sweet. I felt drunk, you know, that emotionally vulnerable, sticky-sentimental kind of drunk, like I wanted to blurt "I love you," and then start boo-hooing.

I was kept from making a complete ass of myself by the appearance of April. She looked matted and scrunched, having just woken up.

"Did you see her?" David demanded.

April nodded and yawned and said, "Yeah. I saw her."

I went to her, reached around into her backpack, and pulled out her bottle of Advil.

"What happened to you?" April wondered. "You look terrible."

"Big rocks hit me in the head," I said. I popped two Advil and swallowed them dry. I handed the bottle to David.

"We ran into some trouble," David explained in his usual Bruce-Willis-laconic style.

"Senna and the Wehrmacht shot us all full of holes. MacCool is deader than Hammer's career. On the one hand guys with machine guns, on the other hand your lovely half sister throwing entire stone fences at us. It was a freaking massacre. And let me just say, I'm hungry."

Etain yelled, "Food! Bring food and drink!" She had that princess voice available when she needed it. You know, that voice you obey before you've had a chance to think about it. She would be great at a crowded Chili's.

April said, "Look, David, Brigid said —"

He cut her off with a look. But it was too late. The name Brigid had the same effect on the king, queen, princess, and assorted druids that the name Elvis would have on the checkout line of a Tennessee Wal-Mart.

"Brigid?" Etain said. "It is the goddess Brigid you speak of?"

David looked impatient, but managed to get a grip on that and said, "Yes, she's in the real . . . in the old world. She made contact with me. She wanted me to do something."

"What?" Fios the druid asked, speaking up for the first time.

David hesitated and suddenly found his own shoes very interesting. Finally, in a soft voice unlike his own, "Long and short of it, I guess she wanted me to kill Senna. Or at least make sure Merlin got hold of her. Make sure the gateway was never opened."

"And you failed," Fios said.

"No," David snapped. "I didn't fail, I never tried."

"If this witch is a gateway between the old world and Everworld then the danger is greater than you can imagine," Fios said. "All the gods will sense the opening. All the gods will know that she has opened the gateway, even though she closed it again. Why did you ignore Brigid's warning? You have brought every curse down upon us. Every evil."

The mood had been bad, now it was worse. No one had anything to say. David couldn't defend himself, of course, that would be making excuses and in his twisted brain that was a no-no.

The fact that Brigid had talked to David gave

him a certain extra importance in these folks'
eyes, I could see that. But the fact that he had not
done what she'd asked him to do, well, that was
making people think he was either stupid or bad.

"Senna's one of us," I said.

April's eyebrows shot up. So did Jalil's. It was
funny there for a moment, the two of them iden-
tically amazed.

"She *was* one of us, anyway," I explained. "Besides, she bewitched David. She put the magic
moves on our boy here."

There was a universal sigh, a sort of unspoken
"Ahh, now I understand" thing from the locals.
That made perfect sense to them. They were pretty
tech-friendly for Everworlders, but they still re-
spected the magic.

"So, what did Brigid say?" Jalil asked April.

Every eye was on April, every ear listened, even
as the food was carried in and David and I and
the remaining Fianna went at it like lions going
after the last wildebeest.

"She said it wasn't too late. She was glad we
were here. Not in Ireland, I mean, but right here
in Merlinshire, although she was sad because she
said a lot of people were likely to die."

"There's some real *Psychic Friends* insights,"
Jalil muttered. "Guys with machine guns pretty
much means people are going to die."

A dozen fairy bowmen came zipping into the room and stood at attention against the wall.

"What else?" David asked April between bites of some kind of meat. "That's all mush — can she help us?"

"She wasn't exactly optimistic, David. She said it's probably too late, that no man's sword or arrow will stop Senna: Her power is too great, Brigid could feel it, that's what she said. She could feel Senna's presence, like a weight on her soul, a darkness on her mind, a shadow over the future. That's pretty close to a direct quote. No man would kill her."

"Yeah. Well, an arrow will sure as hell stop Keith," I said. But my brave words had zero effect. King Camulos looked about three-hundred years old. The stuffing was leaking out of the old boy. Goewynne's cool gray eyes were sad. Fios looked like he'd just gotten the diagnosis and the doctor was talking about how he should make the best of his last few weeks.

Etain seemed shocked, angry, but even she wasn't arguing with the basic pessimism.

David was bummed and guilty, April was bummed and pissed, I was bummed and worried about Etain.

Only Jalil wasn't buying into the gloom and doom.

"I have an idea," he said. "Let's build a tank."

CHAPTER
XV

Senna had recruited us into this madness, she'd chosen us and hijacked us into Everworld to work for her. She'd picked David to be her champion. She'd picked Jalil to be her brains. She'd brought me along to keep the group from ever jelling and coming together. And she'd brought April because Senna is a sadistic bitch and wanted to pay April back for . . . for being a nice, normal, decent girl, I guess.

But now we weren't working for Senna. We were working against her. David's crazy-generalissimo thing was working against her. And so was Jalil's twisted-Spock thing. And April had turned out to be a lot tougher than Senna had thought.

As for me, I was no hero, never had been. But I

wasn't the same guy I had been on that fateful day when Fenrir dragged us all into the deep end of the pool with no water wings. I still see the world as more funny than tragic, I still like a drink, I still admire a babe, I'm still not the ratcheted sphincter that David is. But I wasn't ready to play the screwup anymore.

Keith was my problem, at least to some extent. I wasn't the reason why Senna recruited him, at least I didn't think so: It's just that Keith is registered at the employment agency for the hopeless lava-brains. And yet, I'd had my own involvement with Keith. He'd thought I was like him. That was enough. He thought I was one of him, one of them, and, man, there are few things more disgusting than discovering that some seething little hate machine like Keith thinks of you as a brother.

Plus the little bastard had shot at me.

So I figured at some level Keith was my problem. Let David handle the universe, I'd take care of Keith.

I pitched in with everyone quickly, quickly outfitting Jalil's tank. And when David said we'd divide into two groups, one in the tank that would draw fire, and one that would cruise the roofs and upstairs windows, I said I'd do the tank.

Etain had no idea what was going on with the tank, I guess, but she saw David's expression, the gloomy "Been good to know you, dude" look he gave me. She knew I'd just volunteered to follow MacCool into the Celtic afterlife, so I had my moment of misty-eyed hero worship.

Had to ruin it, of course.

"The tank has a beer cooler, right?" I said.

A fairy came buzzing up the street with the news that the bad guys were at the gates of the village.

"How do they look?" David asked.

The fairy was taken aback by that question. He considered, his shrewd little face twisting into a grimace. "Drunk. I would take them for drunks."

"Was the witch with them?" April asked. "Was Senna there?"

"Not that I could see," the fairy answered carefully. He knew better than to trust his eyes when it came to witches.

"Well, let's do this," David said. And then the cornball grabbed my hand in a manly grip and gave it a manly shake.

"Oh, great, now I'm definitely dead," I said.

David took off with his six fairy archers. Jalil and April headed back to the battlements of the castle. And Etain laid a quick kiss on my cheek.

I was so dead. By all the Unwritten Rules of Movies and Television, I was dead: the reformed bad boy who does the heroic thing at last? I could not be more dead.

"Come on, boys," I said to my own six fairies.

They'd never seen TV, but they seemed to share my own grim assessment. As usual, they looked like real tough twelve-year-olds. They wore livery uniforms, with King Cam's purple-and-green color scheme. They had cute little tin-pot helmets that might almost cause a flying bullet to shrug before it went ahead and tore through their brains and blew gray fairy goo out the back.

We climbed up into the cable car. The tank.

Jalil had commandeered every piece of flat or not-so-flat steel that could be rounded up at short notice. It was roped into place, layered two and three deep around the front of the cable car, creating a kind of dull gray snout. Unneeded track had been torn up and the long I-bars had been hung along the sides with convenient bullet-sized gaps here and there.

Still and all, it was a tank. A San Francisco, Rice-A-Roni tank that could rocket along at an amazing five miles an hour — about as fast as a power walker. Yippee.

I inspected my troops. Fairly idiotic, since under normal circumstances they were the professionals and I was the amateur. But I had a clue as to what we were going into and they had diddly.

"Okay, men. Fairies, I mean. Here's the thing: They have guns, and guns make a whole hell of a lot of noise. Louder than anything you've ever heard before. Don't let the noise rattle you."

Yeah. Why would *bang bang bang* bother anyone?

"And, look, guns can kill you from a long way off, so we wait till I give the signal, all right? No one pokes his head above the armor till I say, otherwise they are going to blow your head right off your shoulders. When we get close enough I'll give the signal, then it's load up your arrow, jump up and shoot, and drop right back down again. This is important: Stay low to load, up and shoot, then get down again. If you stay exposed, you die, period."

As a pep talk it wasn't exactly inspiring. I was depressing myself.

I was driving the cable-tank, but I had a couple of spears and a sword that King Camulos gave me from his own collection. Hard to say how that was going to be useful. But you want to have something.

The cable car was poised at the head of the street, just a few blocks off the main town square.

The cable ran past the station, through the square, across the turntable, then down the main drag to the town gates. About twelve city blocks in all.

I sucked in a deep breath. We wanted to hit the bad guys in the narrow street, not in the square. Time to go.

I grabbed the five-foot-tall lever and jammed it as I'd been shown. Down under the street the gear grabbed the cable and with a wild jerk we were off and cruising, armor rattling like my knees.

Past the station.

"What? No riders waiting?" I muttered nervously. "Okay, then we'll just keep going."

Through the square, and all of a sudden I heard a not-very-distant *popopopopopop*. Someone shooting for fun. Maybe they'd spotted a civilian peeking from behind a shutter. Or maybe they'd just blown a great big hole in David.

Rattling across the square. Time to notice the pigeons. Time to notice the park benches. Time to wonder if the sun ever shined in this place.

And then, into the street, with buildings close on both sides, some almost leaning over us. Two, three-story, some built fairy-scale, some clearly for humans. All shuttered. All silent. Like the town was empty.

Pop. Pop. Pop.

There they were! Twelve, fifteen guys saunter-ing along in a loose gaggle, guns slung every-where, ammo belts, and one of them pulling some rude little wooden cart loaded with green steel ammunition boxes.

They hadn't noticed us yet, and just as they were about to I saw an arrow grow out of one guy's neck. Then a blur of arrows from two high windows. Two guys were down, pincushions, screaming, yelling.

Guns blazed. Men scattered, right, left, hiding under the eves, looking around cautiously, shout-ing insults and challenges.

I saw one of my own fairies peeking. "Stay down!" I yelled. "Jeez, you idiot, I have to be up to drive this thing, what's your excuse?"

Taking my own advice I crouched low, kept my hand on the big lever, but brought most of my body down behind the armor.

David's fairies struck again, this time shooting around a corner from an alley. A dozen arrows flew before the creeps could return fire. And now another of them was staggering around bellow-ing, arrows in both thighs.

A window opened, arrows, machine-gun fire, and a fairy tumbled out and landed on the pave-ment like a sack of cement.

"Shoot the windows!" Keith yelled in sudden

manic inspiration. I recognized his voice. They cut loose, blasting wildly at every window.

But still they didn't shoot at us. I realized why. They saw us; they just didn't know enough about Everworld to know how weird it was that there was a cable car rattling down the street. We were closing fast. Two hundred yards. One-fifty. A hundred, and then . . .

A machine gun opened up on us. The armor rattled like a punk drummer was keeping time with a sledgehammer. The whole rickety car rattled and I dove for the floor, giving my boys the proper example.

Then a bullet found its way through and entered one of my archers in the chest. He looked down at the little red hole and fell straight back.

A fairy jumped up to shoot and spun around, his face a red mess.

"Not yet!" I yelled.

The hammer blows continued, sitting damned ducks, waiting to be killed, sitting here behind too-weak armor, helpless, wanting to shoot back, scared to shoot back, seconds dragging dragging dragging and any second could be the last one.

I was cursing a blue streak, filling the air with nervous, shaky, terrified, half-giggled words. Every word I could think of and making up some new ones. Had to peek, had to see where we were, oh, man, no, let's just cower right here, and gotta do it, up!

I looked and dropped and a stream of lead sliced the space my head had occupied.

I had just four guys now.

"Okay. I'm going to count to three, then shoot and drop," I said. "One. Two. Three!"

Up they popped and bows twanged and they dropped. Say what you will about fairies: They aren't stupid. They learn.

"Ready," I said. "One, two, three!"

Up and shoot and drop.

Up and shoot and drop.

Up and shoot and now I had three archers.

Three dead bodies in the car.

Up and shoot and drop.

We were in them now, right among the bad guys, wild yelling and shooting and cursing, hammer blows and twanging bows and a flying, tumbling steel ball.

Hand grenade!

The explosion ripped a hole in our armor, ripped a four-foot exposure right across the front of Jalil's tank. Fire pouring in, another fairy dead, arrows coming from a high window, and I was yelling, "Keep shooting, keep shooting!" at the last two fairies.

I grabbed a bow myself and fitted an arrow into it. Pathetic, I didn't know what I was doing.

A lurch, the car rocked, a beefy face appeared over the top of the side armor, an angry face, a grown man, for God's sake, trying to stabilize himself long enough to bring his rifle down on me.

I snatched up a spear and stabbed him. A shallow cut on the bottom of his left arm, but he yelled and wobbled uncertainly. My next thrust drew gushing blood from his chest and he fell back.

Then Keith's shrill voice yelling, "Fire in the hole!" and a second grenade went off and I was standing in the side yard looking up at the elm tree with my dad.

"It's the beetles," he said, and I yelled in rage and frustration and grabbed my head with both hands.

"Since when do you care about the yard?" my dad wondered.

CHAPTER
XVI

It was the beetles. Those damned Asian Longhorn beetles that have been going after trees all over the Chicago land, and every time the experts think they've beaten the beetles, the beetles battle back and out come the chain saws. If it wasn't the Dutch Elm disease it was the drought, and look at the lawn. No one wants to work anymore. Used to be neighborhood kids would come around pushing their own lawn mower and do the grass for five bucks, and that was generous. It was almost a relief that summer was over, the pain-in-the-ass yard and all.

I could scream.

I gritted my teeth while beads of sweat popped out all over my forehead despite the fact that there was a definite chill in the air.

Was I dead? Was I dead?

Well, obviously not dead here, not here in the real world, although I might be in some kind of Catholic purgatory wandering along behind my dad as he angrily pointed out the numerous flaws in the perfection of our yard.

He was about a six-pack of the way toward toasted. This was the anger buildup phase. It was late afternoon, I was back from school, the sun was threatening to set way too early, and my dad had obviously bailed out of work early to come home and work out some personal crap with a warm-up six to be followed by a couple quick shots of Jack.

Maybe he'd stop then, but maybe not. If my mom came home in a similar mood it would be one of those nights, the two of them mad-drinking, glaring at each other as they drank to keep even, to pay each other back. Drinking like it was some kind of game of Battleship: I fire a Sam Adams at you! Bastard, you hit my destroyer! Fine, take this martini! You sank my aircraft carrier.

My head was going to explode.

"Need to repaint this area, look at this. The goddam dogs are pissing all over it, and it eats right through the paint. Forget your lazy Saturday, you and me are going to Home Depot, get some paint, and fix this."

"I gotta go," I said. I needed to find David. Jalil. April. Whoever was going to tell me what was happening over there.

"The hell you do. Your mother isn't even home yet."

"I have a thing," I said. My head was buzzy, weirded out, waiting for some slow-motion death to come zap me across the big universal divide. "A school thing."

He laughed. My dad's a screwup, but when he's sober he's okay. He has a sense of humor, at least. "Friday night you better be doing something better than a school thing. What's the name of that girl you were seeing?"

"Jennifer. Yeah, not seeing her anymore," I said. Not much point mentioning that her dad had threatened to kill me if I ever came near him, his daughter, or his wife again. I tried to wink and grin and leer and added, "I have a new target of opportunity in my sights."

"Well, go on," he said, looking deflated and lonely and disgruntled.

I fired up the Cherokee and drove off in search. David first. Not at home. No one at home. I drove to Starbucks where he worked. Not there, but I bought a cup of coffee, and that calmed me down a little. There was a pay phone at the bagel place so I called Jalil. Also not at home. Of course not, it was Friday night and even Jalil had a life. Probably seeing that Japanese chick, Heavy Snow or whatever. Deep Ice. Something.

April. I called her house. Answering machine.

Then I remembered. *"Rent!"* I yelled. The play. April's stupid school play, it was tonight, and I was supposed to be there. I really did have a "school thing." Weird when truth rears its head amid the comforting network of lies.

I looked at my watch. It started at what, eight? An hour. Yeah, April would be there at the auditorium.

I hopped back in the Jeep and pulled away. School parking was always bad, and worse when something was happening. At least tonight's football game was away. I parked on the street, watched by three black guys in full hip-hop regalia. Probably steal my car.

No, we don't think that way anymore, Christopher, I chided myself: That's Keith-ism. Loser-think.

I locked up anyway and pointed my keys like I was turning on the nonexistent alarm. Yeah, that would fool the whole world.

I ran across the street, slowed to a herky-jerky walk across the scruffy prison yard that was our school quad, agitated now, what if April didn't know anything? I mean, what did I think? That she had fallen asleep over in Everworld, just dozed off while we were having our little gun battle?

This was stupid. Unless David was here, too. That's who I needed: David. If he was back on this side then we were both probably dead, which meant no going back at the very least.

"Would that be a bad thing?" I asked myself, and earned a dismissive eye roll from some theater-type girl.

"Hey. Do you know April?" I yelled to her.

She hesitated, stopped. She held the door open for me. "Yeah, I know April."

"Do you know if she's here yet?"

"She probably is," Theater Girl said. She looked me up and down as if assessing whether I was April's boyfriend.

"Well, where would I find her? She's having our baby and she forgot to take her special prenatal vitamins."

Another snotty, dismissive eye roll. "Down the hall, go around down that back area, you know where they always pile all the tables? That leads backstage."

"Thanks. We'll name the baby after you." I ran for it.

April was there all right, in street-hooker costume and slut makeup, practicing a song at half-volume while other kids walked around looking scared or self-important and the theater arts faculty dithered and stormed and yelled orders that no one obeyed.

"April."

She broke off in mid-note. "Christopher. What are you doing here?"

"First let me just say that whole 'want a date, sailor?' look works. I never pictured you doing the fishnets-and-spike-heels thing, but now I'll never picture anything else."

"Always glad to contribute to your little fantasies, Christopher. What's happened?" She took my arm and guided me out of the way, into a dark little corner.

"I think maybe I'm dead," I said.

CHAPTER XVII

"Back up. Last thing I know is I was told to talk to Brigid. Which I did, for all the good that did."

"Yeah, well, things are moving right along. David and I are in the middle of a fairies-versus-Nazis thing that isn't going real well. I think maybe I got blown away."

She stared at me sideways.

"I like the tube top, too," I said.

"Well, we've always wondered what would happen. You know, if something happened to one of us over there. But you know what, you may already be back over there. It's not like you can tell."

"I can tell. At least usually. Not always. Mostly, though, I get this feeling, this, I don't know, this whole kind of checking-out, not-quite-there thing."

She nodded. She knew. But of course she was right, too, we didn't always know for sure.

"Have you seen David?" I asked. "I mean, if I'm dead he may be, too."

"If you're dead over there you're still alive here. You noticed that, right? Hey." She snapped her fingers in my face. "My face is up here. Talk to my face, not my boobs."

"Sorry." I ran my hand back through my hair. "I don't know what to do. I mean, Senna's got Keith over there and a bunch of other inmates from his asylum, and I'm thinking maybe there's some way I can help out, you know?"

"How?"

I shrugged. "I don't know. Sorry, I know I'm, like, messing up your big night. Although basically, just walk out onstage looking like that and you won't have to even sing. Maybe I should go see Brigid. I'm totally lost. I am messed up. I've never been dead before. Normally it's not the kind of thing you have to actually deal with. I mean, you're dead, bye-bye, all done, troubles over, and no school tomorrow. Now it's like, I'm waiting for it to catch up with me. Like there's a time delay, you know? Like it's one of those domino things and we're just waiting for all the dominoes to knock each other down, and then I'm the last domino."

"Okay, listen to me, you're babbling. You're not dead. I mean, you are not dead."

Some guy brushed by and gave me the kind of look you'd give someone who was being reassured he wasn't dead.

"You're not dead. Maybe you are dead over there, I don't know. But maybe it just means you're free. Maybe you won't have to go back. Ever. Maybe it's over for you, that's a good thing, right?"

"What? No. I mean, yes, okay, in theory, but no. You guys are still over there, maybe getting shot right now and I'm over here all safe." I didn't mention the fact that Etain was over there and clearly had a thing for me and it wasn't like beautiful half-elf princesses were just hanging around waiting for me here in the real world.

"Yeah, but you're missing the whole point: If you're dead and that means you're free, then maybe the quicker all of us die, the better. And by the way, I'm still up here. Up here! What is it with you? Do I have to wear a sack?"

"Sorry. I was thinking of Etain."

Then, all at once, every muscle in my body gave way. Like I had no bones. Like I was a jellyfish.

I collapsed at April's feet and rolled over onto my side, not even aware of her spike heels or her legs, just aware of the fact that I could not move.

"Get up," April snapped.

I tried to speak. No sound. Tongue not moving. Lips not moving. Eyes . . . couldn't quite focus them, tried, couldn't . . . I could see her bones. Oh, gross, I could see the bones inside April's legs, she was a skeleton wrapped in bloody muscle, a pulse in the big arteries of her thighs, *woosh*, *woosh* went the blood, right through her body, through the stage floor, equipment, could see through everything, nothing real, everything like some kind of schematic drawing, roughed-in, with details in saturated color, beating hearts all around me, beating hearts floating inside ghostly bodies.

I couldn't move. Paralyzed.

Oh, Jesus, it was happening.

Far-off voices yelling. Hands lifting me up, a sack of dirt, a side of beef, no feeling except very slow and far away and nothing to see but the insides of my eyelids with jumpy animated figures like those old, old Mickey Mouse cartoons, everyone jerking and then slowing, all in rhythm to the rust-red hearts.

April was there. Two Aprils. And Etain. And some old dude with a beard and a doctor with curly hair and nurses and bright fluorescent lights and candles. Ceiling tile. Stone arches. Needles. Tubes. Chanting.

And a creature made out of light. Cold, hard light that shined from far, far away.

Etain?

No, I saw Etain now, more clearly, and the light was beside her, casting no shadows, a light that was felt more than seen.

Goewynne. The elf queen.

And yes, Etain, too, but her light was not so bright. And now April, but dressed in her mismatched Everworld duds.

Damn, I really preferred the tube top.

"I was almost dead," I said in a raspy, unrecognizable voice.

"Yes," Etain said.

"We sewed up the shrapnel holes we could see," April said wearily. "But there was internal bleeding. I . . . you know, I'm not exactly a doctor. And their regular doctors here are, you know . . . not exactly doctors either. You were unconscious the whole time, but then, all of a sudden your breathing got very weird. You started shaking. I didn't know what to do."

I took a deep breath and realized I hurt in more places than I could count. "I saw Mom. You know . . ."

Etain said, "Yes, my mother used her powers and the magic summoned by the druids, and together with April's knowledge, your life was saved."

"Tell her thanks," I whispered.

"Sleep now."

"No. No," I murmured. "I messed up the show for you, April."

"That's okay, Christopher."

Etain laid a cold cloth across my forehead and held my hand. April smoothed my hair. And I thought, *Well, at least this hospital has great-looking nurses.*

And I woke up in a real hospital where the real nurses didn't look anywhere near as beautiful.

I woke up in the real world again, happy, healthy, hungry, and a huge frustration to the doctors who had found nothing wrong with me at all — aside from the fact that I'd almost died.

CHAPTER
XVIII

My real-world body was fine. My Everworld body was not so good. Goewynne and the blue druids did what they could, but I wasn't the only wounded person. A series of rooms had been outfitted with cots and turned into a sort of hospital. A weird-ass hospital run jointly by Dr. April, Goewynne, the druids, and the lovely Etain.

April ran around insisting that everyone boil instruments and clean the sheets and wash the floors and stop picking their noses while working on open wounds. At the end of each rotten day she would grab a couple of hours sleep and, once across, would take her most recent questions to the university medical library for answers. I was pretty sure she'd be doing heart transplants before long.

Etain was the chief nurse. She held hands and

read poems and wrote letters and telegrams for the wounded men and fairies. She changed bandages and gave sponge baths. She gave me a sponge bath and it was a pretty clear indication of how badly I was messed up that I didn't even leer, let alone make any kind of a move.

Goewynne worked with the druids, coming in to do some chanting and laying on of hands and some signing and some stuff involving candles and various stones, herbs, weeds, flowers, and stuff you don't want to think about.

Their big thing was "purging." They were very big on purging, which at first I took to be some kind of harmless mumbo jumbo. Guess again. Let me just say this: When the druids give you a laxative, they aren't kidding around. Phillips Milk of What? Forget that, man, try the Nasty Blue-gray Druid Shake.

Somehow this melding of primitive herbal medicine and primitive real medicine and mumbo jumbo deedly-deedly-deedly psycho wand-waving medicine all worked together.

After a week I was able to get up and totter around the hallways leaning on Etain's arm. I was eating bread and soup pretty well. And I was starting to think that beer was in my future in a few more days.

But things weren't going well overall. There

were thirty-one people in the hospital. Now there were even women who had been attacked and savaged by Senna's army, which now occupied the town and had the castle entirely surrounded and cut off.

The good guys had taken out a lot of her people, but she seemed to be restocking with men and ammo. Our spies thought she might have thirty guys now. They hadn't figured out how to get over the castle walls yet, but it was just a matter of time. They'd tried to climb over using ladders, but their guns were not as big an advantage in that situation. Hard to shoot through a rock slit while you're hanging on to a ladder with one hand.

David and Jalil's Double-F army — Fairies and Fianna — repelled the attempt and did it in such a way as to discourage another attempt. Jalil had figured out how to brew up some seriously awful sulphuric acid. He was now a god to the druids.

Since then it had settled down to a siege. Senna's creeps had the town pretty well under their control. They had enslaved the town's people. The townspeople were used to perform hard labor, building bunkers to create machine-gun nests covering the main roads. They were robbed of everything they had. They were used for target practice.

The hospital was not a happy place.

David and Jalil came to see me. David was weary, bruised, bandaged. Jalil was no better.

"Hey, Christopher. How you doing?"

"Except for Etain's and April's constant sexual demands on me, I'm fine," I said.

David managed a fleeting smile.

"How's the war going, General?"

"One of the people in the town, a woman, got loose and made it to the gate. We got her in, just barely. She had information. She heard Senna and Keith and a couple of the others, some guy called Graber, talking. Senna's trying to get some of her people back in the real world to line up some heavy hardware: mortars at least, maybe cannon. Keith and Graber want her to send them back across to the real world. Senna says no. She says the guys on the other side, the real-world guys, have a line on some heavy stuff. I don't need to tell you that if they bring in even one mortar it's pretty much all over. Let alone hard-core artillery pieces."

"Why do Keith and this other guy want to go back?" I wondered.

"They figure whoever comes up with the heat to take us is going to be the big man among the Sennites," Jalil explained.

"Sennites? They have a name now?"

"I guess so. Is that water? You mind?" David reached for my pitcher.

"Help yourself. So the next question is, why doesn't Senna send them back across the divide to get whatever she needs?"

David shrugged. "I don't know. Jalil has some theories."

I gave Jalil a sour look. "He always does."

Jalil said, "Look, this name came up: Mr. Trent. He may be the guy on the other side who is going to help Senna get the heavy ordnance. That's your guy, right? The one at the copy shop?"

"My guy? I don't think he's exactly my guy. I tried to put Keith in jail because Keith was threatening me. And why? Because Trent told him to, that's why." I peered at David and then groaned. "Oh, man, you're kidding, right? He'd shoot me on sight if he could."

David nodded. "Maybe. Maybe not. Thing is, April can't do it — she's a girl and they don't trust girls. Me, I'm a Jew; Jalil's black. He's not going to let either of us get close. Besides, the other you, real-world Christopher has already agreed to go along with the plan."

"Yeah, well, real-world Christopher is an idiot if he's agreed to go up and talk to Trent again. What am I supposed to do? Just ask him whether he's got any tanks for Everworld?"

"No, actually, you're going to shoot Jalil."

"Excuse me?"

"With blanks. Better be with blanks," Jalil said darkly. "When you get back across, you double-check that you've pried the slugs out."

"I'm not shooting anyone."

"With your dad's gun," David said. "Trent sees you shooting a black guy. He figures he owns you after that."

"My dad doesn't let me borrow his gun to kill people. He's very strict about that."

"That's the same thing real-world you said. I mean, to the word," Jalil marveled.

"April will supply fake blood, you know, theater blood," David said. "She'll do some screaming and all. You do the shooting and throw in some well-chosen words . . ." He gave me a significant look.

"N-word," Jalil supplied. "It'll be like old times for you, Christopher."

"You just need to pry the slugs out of the bullets and jam cardboard in," David said.

"I want to emphasize that part and make sure we're real damn clear: Take out the slug," Jalil said. "Take out all the slugs."

David nodded. "That would be the main thing not to forget."

"Take out the slugs," Jalil repeated.

"You guys are crazy."

"Yes, we are," Jalil said. "We're desperate. Mortar shells will sail right over the big walls out there and all the chanting druids in the world aren't going to stop them from blowing everything in here apart. They have Senna's magic stalemated for now, but they aren't real good at stopping bullets."

"When am I supposed to do this?" I asked. "And why are you bothering me if you already have real-world Christopher all lined up?"

David put the water cup back. "April needs to give you the fake exploding blood sacks and we can't find real-world you."

"He's probably running for Wisconsin about now," I said.

"Tell real-world you to call April at her home, first thing," Jalil said.

"Yeah. And fast. Let me put it this way: Go to sleep, Christopher. April?!" He yelled her name and she appeared, harassed, hurrying, eyes rimmed red from lack of sleep.

"Here. Goewynne made it. She says it will put you right to sleep." She handed me a tin cup full of something that smelled like old-lady perfume mixed with fertilizer.

I glared but what could I do? I was useless here, still too weak to move. I had to do what I could, right? I drank the drug down in one gulp and tried not to shudder at the taste.

"So you're saying real bullets?" I said.

"Pry out the slugs," Jalil said.

"Extra big slugs, got it."

"Screw you, too."

And then I was across.

CHAPTER
XIX

Real-world me was not running for Wisconsin. Real-world me's phone was accidentally off the hook. Real-world me was having a jumpy fit waiting around while it got dark outside and no one contacted me.

I hung up the phone and eight seconds later April called.

"Where the hell have you been?"

"You've been looking for me to give me some blood sacks," I said. "I'm psychic."

"Do you have the thing?"

The thing was in my pocket. I had already pried the slugs out and stuck wads of chewed-up cardboard in to replace them. Then I'd checked the whole thing over about six times.

"Oh yeah, baby, I have the thing you need. Uh-huh."

"Are you actually standing there leering and rotating your pelvis like some kind of arthritic Elvis impersonator?"

I froze. "No. Of course not. How did you know?"

"I'm on a cell phone. I just drove up, for which I'll be grounded, by the way, since it isn't exactly my car. I'm right outside on the sidewalk."

I looked through the window. She was under a dim streetlight. I hung up and went outside. Went back inside to grab a jacket. Back out.

"You know this is a total screwup in the making, right? You know we're the *Titanic* Twins and there's a big-ass iceberg out there waiting for us," I said.

April sighed, but in agreement not exasperation. "Come on, let's get going. No, let's walk. I'm not getting a bullet hole in my dad's Mercedes. Besides, there's never any parking."

"Any acting tips for me?"

"Don't act. Be in the moment," she said, then laughed. "That's why you get the blood sacks. Jalil will have his own to pop and look like a bullet wound. But we figured you should have some blood spattered all over you. The blood will do the acting for you."

She handed me a sort of little pellet, a tiny water balloon.

"Hold it in your left hand, right? No, like this.

Gun in your right hand. *Bang, bang, bang.* Squeeze the blood — it'll spray back on your shirt and face."

"You know, when you talk all Hollywood like this, it so totally gets me hot."

She didn't laugh. "Christopher, I think Etain may actually like you. No one can imagine why, but she does. So why are you going all lizard with me?"

This was cool news. My heart actually skipped a few beats. That happens fairly frequently, but it's always been from terror before.

"What, I can't have different girls in different universes?"

"Focus on this, okay?" she said. "We don't get to retake the scene."

"I'm trying not to focus," I grumbled. It was another five blocks to downtown where we were supposed to enact our little idiot play. My palms were already sweating.

I looked in the bright windows of the houses we passed. Way too many framed posters of old French advertisements, way too much Pottery Barn. Nice, nice TV light. The comforting blue glow. Oh, man, I would so like to be watching TV.

Downtown was quiet; it usually is. I was in that forcing-myself-to-breathe thing you get into when the dread is trying to choke you to sleep before you do something stupid. Not looking forward to this.

"Okay, I have to split off," April said. "You okay?"

"Sure. You okay?"

"No," she said. "It's different when it's here. This is the real world. It's not right. This crap should all be over there, not here." Then she walked away.

The plan was simple enough. Trent parked his car in a back alley a block away from his shop. We were supposed to wait for him to lock up the shop and head toward his car. David would be watching and call me on April's cell phone, which she had loaned me. Then Jalil and I would go into our act. Mr. Trent would happen along in time to witness our little play. I'd be all freaked out and beg him to help me escape. April would wander by and do some screaming. Trent would figure now that he had seen me do the Big Crime he would have me cold. I'd be welcomed into the warm arms of the psycho-freak fraternity.

And that's pretty much how it worked out.

Pretty much.

Jalil and I waited two hours, shivering in a dark alley, avoiding the dubious looks of students taking the alley shortcut to campus.

At last April's Nokia rang.

"Yeah?"

"He's on the move."

I put the phone back on my hip and wished my heart would slow down. "Okay, man, we're on," I said.

"You took out the slugs, right?" Jalil asked me for roughly the two-hundredth time.

"Okay. Count to ten. One. Two. Three. Screw it. Here goes."

I started yelling at Jalil, and Jalil started yelling at me, the two of us going at it like Pat Buchanan and Louis Farrakhan on *The Jerry Springer Show*. I was up in his face, he was up in mine.

A slight noise. Someone entering the alley.

I drew my gun, shaky, shaky, and Jalil jumped back and yelled something unpleasant.

"Stop it! Stop it!" a woman's voice cried.

What?

A middle-aged woman wearing a peasant dress. "What are you doing?" she cried.

And then, right behind her, Mr. Trent.

"Do it!" Jalil hissed.

BANG. Pause. BANG.

I fired. Jalil staggered back. The woman screamed. April, coming out of nowhere, screamed. I totally forgot the blood pellet. Too much screaming.

I hid my face and pushed past the woman.

And Trent, wild-eyed, said, "Do the woman, you can't leave a witness."

I shook my head violently. I was doing a pretty good job of playing the hyped, frazzled, stunned killer.

Trent gripped me hard and pulled me into him. "Do the woman, you moron, or she'll ID me, too, and I'll have to testify against you."

Yeah, kind of like we planned.

"I'll take care of it," he said.

And in my dazed-idiot state I said, "Okay," having no freaking idea what he was talking about. Till I saw him pull out his own gun.

When the brain is frozen, sometimes sheer dumb instinct is all you've got. Sheer dumb instinct swung on Trent, caught him with my own gun barrel under the chin.

Jalil jumped up off the ground and came running. Trent was staggered, fumbling to get his own gun out, and I was pretty sure he had not pried the slugs out of his bullets.

Jalil took a flying leap and down went the three of us. The woman ran for the street screeching. April came running up. David was crossing the street. Cops would be there in two minutes.

I had Trent's gun hand and Jalil pried the weapon out of his hand.

David loomed up. "Get his keys out of his pocket."

I did as I was told, glad to have someone tell me what to do.

The four of us hustled the future Führer into his rusty old Econoline van and kicked and shoved him into the dirty, crowded back.

"Plan's working pretty well," I said, wincing as I banged my shin on a wooden crate.

"Does this stuff wash out?" Jalil wondered, looking at the bloody mess on his shirt.

"What are you punks after?" Mr. Trent managed to ask around his split lip.

"I'm trying to raise money for the school band by selling magazine subscriptions," I said. "And by the way, this is your gun I'm pointing at you, not mine. I shoot you, you won't get up like Jalil here."

David cranked the wheezy engine, April in the passenger seat buckled her seat belt, and we lurched away just as the sound of sirens got really loud.

"I just want to say, hell of a plan, guys, just a hell of a fine plan. It's like Mission: Im-Freaking-possible. Why did I let you two talk me into this? Am I stupid?"

It took about ten minutes of driving around without a clue, me bitching nonstop, before one of us — Jalil, naturally — noticed what we were sitting on.

"These are crates, man," he said. "Look: stencil markings."

"I can't see anything."

The back windows of the van were painted black. The only light came from the windshield.

We found a place to stop, in the parking lot of a twenty-four-hour Dominick's grocery store on Green Bay. It still wasn't light in the back, so April went into the store and bought a pair of small flashlights while we all sat and stared at Trent.

"What's up with you?" David asked the man.

"You get nothing from me but name, rank, and serial number," Trent snapped.

"Rank? What rank?" David asked. "We have your name, you don't have a rank, and you don't have a serial number. What are you, an idiot?"

"Is that Jew I smell?"

Before David could answer, April returned. Using the flashlights and the tire iron we found in the back, we opened one crate. A row of shells lay in a molded plastic form.

There was a long moment of silence, and a slow exhalation.

I looked at David and Jalil, both smirking. "Don't even look smug, you two. It doesn't count if the plan works by accident."

In the next crate we found a mortar, broken down in pieces. And then a second crate of mortar rounds.

"Now what?" April asked. "We can't just dump this stuff somewhere."

"Sure we can," Jalil said with his slow, reptilian smile forming. "I know exactly where we can dump all this stuff."

Later that night the FBI office in Chicago got a call from a pay phone. They discovered a parked van outside their building. The van contained a hog-tied Nazi and a large cache of illegal weapons.

CHAPTER
XX

Everworld me was getting better. I could walk normally. I could eat. The fever was gone. I was well enough to bathe myself. Which was a shame because I was also well enough that I'd have enjoyed having Etain give me a sponge bath.

See, there's the Catch-22: If you might enjoy it, you don't get it. Pretty well sums up life as we know it.

The hospital was no longer as full. The men and fairies had learned how to keep their heads down. And for now Senna was stopped at the castle gates. So Etain's visits with me could take a little longer. Mostly she asked about the real world. Mostly about stuff I didn't know much about.

"Light has a particular speed, then? And how do you know it doesn't go faster or slower depending on whether the spirits are agitated or calm?"

"I don't know. Scientists do this stuff. I just get tested on it. Doesn't mean I understand it."

"One hundred and eighty-six thousand miles per second," Etain marveled. "Faster even than one of your bullets."

"Yeah. And faster than sound. That's why you see the flash of a gun and don't hear the sound till a second or so later."

"Is that true, then?" she said excitedly. "Come, let us go to the walls and see."

"You want to get shot at so we can see if light travels faster than sound? I'm thinking, no."

She smiled. "There is something in what you say."

Mostly that was it: a lot of talk about cars and internal combustion engines and jet engines and medicine and space shuttles and DNA and phones and television and why *Survivor* had been a hit and so on.

But that was okay, she liked talking about the real world and I liked talking to her about anything as long as she'd sit close to my bed and look beautiful and smell great and be nice to me.

When you've spent a couple of months wandering around lost in Weird World, running from one evil mess to the next, and finally getting up close and personal with a hand grenade, you are desperately, giddily, puppy-dog grateful for a pretty girl who'll sit there and give you a lively sense of what you're living for.

But still, nothing had gotten personal. No kiss, no grope, no exchanges, shall we say. I knew I had to get up serious nerve. But things were so nice I just didn't want to mess it up by trying for the next level. Plus, of course, there was the omnipresent fear of Etain's fairy bodyguard.

But eventually I had to make some kind of a play. I was right on the edge of being the kind of guy some chick's father would approve of. That couldn't last.

It was to be my last night in the hospital. The last time when Etain could legitimately come to see me as my nurse, without it being some big thing. She mentioned that she'd be by after supper. She mentioned it casually. But she blushed when she mentioned it casually, so I had my hopes up pretty high.

As it happened, she came by earlier than usual. Two hours earlier. I figured, hey, if she's showing up two hours early she must actually like me. Clearly the time had come to make a move.

She asked me how I was doing. She asked me

how I felt. And with the grace and subtlety for which I am justly famous, I said, "So, Etain, on another topic entirely, do you have a boyfriend?"

"A boyfriend?"

"A squeeze. You know, some guy you're involved with."

"A betrothed?"

Hmmm. "Okay, sure, a betrothed."

"I was betrothed," she said without too much sadness. "He was a prince of Blackpool. But alas, he died. He was gored by a boar and infection set in, the wound mortified."

"Alas," I said with some genuine sympathy. When you get blowed up real good you discover you have a lot of sympathy for anyone who's suffered something similar.

"He might have been saved with April's mold," Etain said thoughtfully.

I nodded. "Yeah. April needs to see about patenting her mold. The girl's looking at some serious cash flow."

"April is an inspiration," Etain said sincerely. "The druids fairly worship her."

April's mold was crude penicillin. Not all that hard to grow in a land where it seemed to be damp pretty much all the time. Between boiling everything in sight and demanding that everyone wash their hands and introducing antibiotics, April had moved medical science forward about a thousand years. She had used up her stock of Advil, but now she was at work figuring out how to make aspirin.

"Yeah, well, watch out for April: She'll have you all eating broccoli and saying the Rosary if you're not careful. But enough about her. The thing is, if we don't all get killed, is there any way you and I could see each other?"

"Do we not see each other now?"

"Yeah, but I mean see as in 'see.' Hang. Do things together. Date."

"You mean court?" She laughed, trying to cover for a blush that reddened her cheeks and extended down her neck.

"Yeah, it's like courting, but less serious. I mean courting is about getting married, right? Dating is like courting except you don't get married. I mean, maybe in Utah you get married, but mostly not."

"No?"

I shrugged. "Well, no, probably. I mean, someday. I guess." The fever seemed to be coming back. "But what you do is you go to places and have fun. You take a drive in the car. Or the . . . horse. You go horse riding together. You catch a movie or possibly a druid ritual, depending on what's showing, or you grab a burger. You talk about stuff."

"Just talk?" she asked.

I hesitated. Was that a signal of some kind? Was Etain a couple of steps ahead of me? "Talk, mostly," I said cautiously.

"Do you never embrace?"

"Embrace?"

"Do you never kiss?"

Yes, yes, she was a couple of steps ahead of me.

She leaned close, leaned right across me, and kissed me on the lips.

Right away it wasn't right. I knew what I expected. I'd spent a few hundred hours thinking about kissing Etain, and this wasn't it.

I felt strange, disturbed. I felt as if I was getting sicker. As if someone was drugging me, that was it, like someone had slipped me a Demerol or something.

I tried to pull away. But it was too late.

I opened my eyes. And now I was too far gone even to register surprise. Of course it was Senna's face, Senna's eyes so close to my own. Laughing, contemptuous eyes.

"Hi, Christopher," she said as she drew back. "Long time no see."

I felt muzzy, fuzzy anger and fear way, way down inside me. But on the surface of my mind, in the brain that actually controlled my rawest emotions, my actions, I felt only helpless surrender.

I knew it was Senna now. Senna, the shapeshifter. Senna the witch. I knew what Senna was. I knew exactly what she was doing. And still I reached for her. Still I leaned to kiss her.

"One more to seal the bargain," she breathed.

And I was lost.

CHAPTER
XXI

"You'll see this is for the best, Christopher," she told me. "All this fighting and killing has to stop. Too many people are getting hurt. And why? Because David wants to play the hero. You know it's true."

A grain of truth. Not the real truth, not the complete truth, but a grain.

"Everworld is a mess," Senna went on. She was pacing beside my bed, alternately wringing her hands slowly, glancing nervously toward the door, and favoring me with syrupy pity looks. "Mad creatures forever killing one another. It needs to be organized. I mean, how is it ever going to become a decent place unless someone comes along to guide them toward the kind of life that we all believe in?"

Yes, that was true, Everworld was a mess.

She was working on me, I knew that. Part of me was still there, functioning. Part of me was still skeptical, still aware that I was being fed a line of b.s.

But that part of me was wrapped in gauze, a mummy. That part of me mumbled and shuffled and blinked nearsightedly, unable to quite focus.

"I know you want to support your friends, but aren't I your friend, too?" Senna asked. "We were close once, Christopher, before David came along and pushed you out of my life."

Is that what happened? Kind of. No, no, it was more . . . that wasn't it. But kind of, right?

"David and Jalil are in this together, you know that, don't you? Jalil thinks he's so great. He thinks he's better than you. You must know that. You must know that secretly, behind your back, he laughs at you."

She was lying, wasn't she? She had tried to kill me. Jalil had saved my life more than once.

But there was truth in what she said, too. Of course there was truth. David was a jumped-up martinet. Jalil was an arrogant smart-ass.

"And what about April? She's just a tease, Christopher. I mean, you're not stupid, Christopher; you know it's not an accident when she flashes a little leg or some cleavage at you. You know she's playing with you, and there's no chance she'll ever be yours. No, no, it's Jalil she wants. You know, some girls are like that."

Jalil and April? I searched my memory, but memory was a slow, slow, slow-loading file. The software all frozen up, couldn't quite reach it, couldn't quite get it to boot up.

"Nice boy like you, Christopher, you don't have a chance with April, not with that smart-ass Jalil in there, taking what should be yours."

No, that was . . . that wasn't right. But it was true, wasn't it? April did like Jalil. And of course he liked her, of course, who wouldn't? And everyone knows how they are. Everyone knows.

Senna was still close. Close enough that I could smell the perfume of her; God, she smelled so sweet, so beautiful. The most beautiful girl in the world, a movie star, a shining angel. I wanted her. She cared about me, oh she didn't always show it, but she cared about me.

"Etain is the same way," Senna said. "But she wants David. She wants to be taken, you know, taken by a strong, dominant, aggressive man. And David will do it. He'll do it."

I blinked. No. No, there was no truth there. Was there? No. Senna was just wrong. That wasn't it at all.

Senna didn't know Etain.

That fact stuck. As loopy as I was, that fact was

solid: Senna had not been here these last weeks, she didn't know Etain.

Senna peered closely at me, looked at my eyes with the detachment of an optometrist checking for glaucoma. She pressed her lips together, angry at herself, sensing that she'd played her cards wrong. Then she relaxed into a smile.

"I can give you Etain," she said playfully, teasing. "That's what you want, isn't it?"

She was changing tactics, changing approaches. Trying to come at me from a different direction.

Come on, Christopher, shake free. Shake free.

"We'll get rid of David and Jalil," Senna whispered. She laid her hand on my arm, on the bare skin, and I felt a shiver run up and down my spine.

My brain, my memory, just surfacing, just coming up for air, just emerging from the smothering water, was thrust back down, pushed hard, back under, back under.

Couldn't hold on. She was talking again, talking to me close, so close, so beautiful, and I was slipping, further than ever.

A song was in my head, a song going round and round. Santana?

* * *

"Better leave your lights on,
Because there's a monster.
There's a monster living under my bed,
Whispering in my ear."

"Help me, Christopher. You want to help me,
Christopher, and it will all be yours. Etain will be
yours. Etain will be yours forever."

And then she was Etain, she was Etain, and she
was pressing her body close, covering my face in
hot kisses. Etain. Etain.

"It's time to go," Etain breathed in my ear.

"Go where?" I mumbled.

"You must go," she whispered.

There's a monster, Christopher, a monster,
whispering in your ear. "Wha . . . where?"

"To the gate of the castle. It needs to be opened.
You would be my hero, Christopher."

Not Etain. It was . . .

"Be my hero, Christopher, and you'll have me,
all of me without reservation. Go to the castle
gate. You must open the gate. Take your sword.
Lift up the crossbar. Then cut the drawbridge rope.
Do those things, Christopher, do them and I am
yours forever and ever."

Etain kissed me again. No, the monster. Etain.

"Now, go."

The word "go" snapped in my head. Electric. Irresistible. I stood. I fumbled for my sword.

"Go, Christopher. Be my true hero."

I went.

CHAPTER
XXII

I closed the door behind me. Stepped into the hallway. A passing fairy nodded at me, the respectful nod due to a wounded fighter.

What was I doing? Open the gate. Drop the drawbridge.

Why?

Um . . .

Open the gate, drop the drawbridge.

The monster whispering in my ear. But Etain was no monster. Etain was not Etain.

That damned David. Freaking glory dog, that's what he was. Him and Jalil working together to cut me out. Laughing at me behind my back.

Jalil wanted Etain. Or was it David? One of them. Both of them? Etain and April and everyone.

Down the hall. Down the turning, turning stairs. Like Sleeping Beauty's castle. I'm Sleeping

Beauty, that's what it is, I'm sleeping, way down here inside my own brain.

My sword. I was wearing the sword old King Camulos had given me.

What was going to happen to the king and to Goewynne? Oh, it would be okay, Senna would be decent to them. She wasn't going to hurt anyone, not the monster, not the monster Senna.

Out into the courtyard. Weird, fresh air. Fresh cold night air. First fresh night air in a long time. It was good to be out of the hospital.

Still a little shaky, though. Shaky. Weak. Walking like an action figure, stiff, unnatural.

Like a puppet.

Across the courtyard. There was the gate, massive timbers bound with iron straps. Two things: the inner gate and the drawbridge beyond it. Had to open both.

If Keith and the Sennites just made it across the drawbridge but ran into a locked gate, they were screwed. There was a narrow passage between the drawbridge and the inner gate, high walls looming over it all, firing positions everywhere. Come in the drawbridge and get held up by the inner gate, you were toast: crammed into a space twenty feet long and six feet wide with fairy archers above you, pouring arrows into you. Or worse, some of Jalil's acid bath.

It had to be both or Keith couldn't come in. But if they were both open, that would be okay. Then the little psycho could come in, run through the gauntlet of arrows.

Keith. Senna. It was Senna. Senna was Etain and Etain loved me, wanted me to save her.

The gate. A fairy and a man on guard. Had to take out the fairy first. Take him by surprise, otherwise he'd be too fast. Then the man. The fairy, then the man.

How? If I drew my sword wouldn't they freak? What was I supposed to do, take them both on? That wasn't me, man. Not me, man.

Don't be afraid, Christopher, it's all going to be fine. Etain will be yours. Happy. Everything as it should be.

The man was looking at me. Bored. A guard pulling late-night duty.

"Hi," I said. "Hey, you're probably a real expert and me, I don't know anything about swords. What's the handle part thing here called, this part?"

I drew my sword hesitantly, unsure, an amateur handling a complex tool. The soldier smiled, smug and superior. The fairy ignored us both.

I drew and slammed the handle directly back into the fairy's face. Then I swung the blade in an arc, aiming for the man's neck, but he was quick.

He jumped back and the blade sliced him across the chest, right through the leather jerkin, biting flesh and spraying blood.

The fairy was staggered. The man just surprised. He was trying for his own sword. I kicked him where no man wants to be kicked. I swung my sword pommel again and caught him hard on the side of the head. Down went the Fiannan. I spun and stabbed at the fairy and the blade point hit bone. The fairy fell on his back and I could see he was out cold.

"Let's see David do any better than that," I crowed, wishing Etain were there to see how well I'd done; man, she'd be proud.

The gate's crossbar was heavy. Like a tree. I had to crouch under it and use my legs to lift. Slide it away. Slide and heave till it toppled off. It still blocked the left gate, but I'd be able to open the right door all right.

I pulled with all my strength and the gate swung inward.

Now, there, a big pulley holding the spooled rope. The rope taut up to the guide that led it to the drawbridge.

"Who goes there?" a man's voice yelled from above, up on the wall.

I swung my sword hard and sliced through the rope.

"Alarm! Alarm! To the gate! Alarm!"

A spear flew and nicked my left arm and stuck into the ground and the drawbridge didn't drop, it still stood, balanced. I ran straight at it, yelling, hit it with all my weight and bounced back.

I landed on my back, winded. The drawbridge creaked and slowly, slowly, then faster, fell away.

I rolled over, winded, on hands and knees, tried to stand, tried to get up, saw a rush of fairies rushing at me, zooming, blurring.

Then behind me the sharp sounds of the old world. *Pop. Pop. PopPopPopPop.* Red flowers appeared in the fairies' chests and they fell.

I turned, bleary, lost now that I'd done all I'd been told to do, confused. I caught a Doc Marten in the head.

I was in the shower. "No!"

Staggered back against the cool tile, rocked, uncomprehending. CNN Breaking News: Christopher bewitched by Senna. Christopher gets everyone killed.

"No way, no way." I denied it, but no way to deny it. Everworld me was there with an update. Everworld me had been taken over by Senna, a wholly owned subsidiary.

But not real-world Christopher. The fuzziness, the confusion, none of it affected me now. Now I could see it all with perfect clarity.

I had handed victory to Senna. She would kill us all. David and Jalil and April. And Goewynne and the king. And all the brave Fianna and the fairies and the druids, too.

And Etain.

I turned off the water, numb. What could I do? What had I done? What could I do now?

I wrapped a towel around myself and ran for the phone. I grabbed it and dialed David's number. *Ring. Ring.*

Someone picked it up. Not David. My brother picking up the extension.

"Dammit, get the hell off the phone right now or I'll beat you till you can't walk!" I screamed, panicked, hysterical.

I couldn't be the cause of all those deaths, no, no, I couldn't be the one, I couldn't make Etain die. Had to be some way.

Ring. Ring.

"Levin residence, talk to me."

David!

"It's Christopher."

"Yeah?"

"David. David, man. David, I . . ." All at once I was sobbing, unable to control my voice.

"Calm down, Christopher. Take a breath."

I took a breath. Took another. "I screwed everyone, David. Senna got to me. I opened the gate.

Senna got to me. I let Keith into the castle, David."

"What?"

"David, man, they're in. They're in the castle."

A long pause. Then, "Yeah, they are," David said. "Yeah. Something happened. I'm down, Christopher."

David had just had his own breaking news. Everworld David was down, at least unconscious. Maybe dying. And now, thanks to my own recent close call, we knew what for so long we'd wondered about: Death in Everworld was death all the way around.

Call-waiting on David's line.

"I better get that," he said grimly.

He clicked over to the other line and I waited, trying to breathe, waiting to fade, waiting for death to reach me across the gap.

A long wait. Then David was back.

"That was Jalil. He was in and out. Unconscious, but then he thinks maybe he regained consciousness, he doesn't know for sure. You know how it is."

"Yeah. Jesus, David. I'm sorry. She was there in my room. I thought she was Etain. I mean, she was Etain. She got to me."

"I know how it is, Christopher. No one knows better than me. Jalil says it looks bad. He doesn't know what happened to either of us. It's chaos over there."

"April?"

"She hasn't called."

"So maybe she's fine."

"Or dead," David said. "Don't give up. Don't wimp out on me."

I realized I was crying into the phone and that David could hear me.

"Let's go see Brigid," he said.

"Okay, man. I'm okay. I'm okay."

"I'll be there in five."

And I guess I was there when he drove up. I guess because Everworld me had just woken up in a world of hurt.

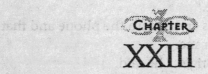

CHAPTER

XXIII

I was alive, but felt like I'd rather not be.

I was lying on my side. A dead man was sprawled beside me. Two dead fairies, one draped right across me. Dead people all around.

They thought I was dead. I'd been dragged and dumped with the dead bodies. And just then a druid and a servant from the castle came shuffling along carrying another dead man. They were supervised by a jeering, swaggering punk I'd never seen before. He had a Kalashnikov propped on his hip. He was eating a roll of some kind.

Everything was lit by fire. Night had fallen, but the village was burning, and the glow of orange reached up to dim the stars.

I closed my eyes to slits. I felt the thud as the body was slung toward me. I saw another of Senna's boys, a big bruiser of a guy, head scraped bald, tattooed, a pair of automatic pistols in a leather belt, a machine pistol in his left hand, dragging a dead fairy along by the hair.

The punk said, "Hey, compadre, you ain't gotta be carrying them yourself. Get a couple of the prisoners to do it."

"The little ones don't weigh much," the big man said.

"No, but they're fast," the punk said. Then, with a laugh added, "When they're alive. Ha-ha-ha, not too fast now."

The two of them walked off laughing at this wit and embellishing the joke further. Variations on the theme of "dead people are slow."

I figured now was the time.

I felt for my sword. Gone. But the nearest fairy still carried his sword, more like a dagger, really. I slid it from his belt, whispering an apology for robbing the dead.

I slithered across the corpses, sick at heart, sick in every way, crawled and slithered across the drawbridge. If I was seen I'd have to run. Out-run bullets. No problem. But better than waiting around till someone noticed I wasn't exactly dead.

No *popopop*. No explosion of pain in my back. I got up and ran. Ran and ran, down through the burning town, gagging on the swirling smoke. I tripped over a charred body, got up and kept running. I was crying from smoke and weak rage. What was happening back up in the castle? What were Senna's monsters doing to my friends and Etain?

One thing was sure: David was either dead or unconscious. Couldn't pawn this off on David. Not his turn to play hero, not this time. This was on me. But what the hell was I going to do? No gun, no army, nothing but a knife.

This was so screwed up. And it was my fault. I should have been able to resist Senna. Should have been able to keep her from playing with my mind. All the times I'd made fun of David for being her sock puppet. And now whose hand was up my butt? I was the new star of Senna's very own *Sesame Street*.

I saw a column of men approaching and ducked into a black, charred, smoking alley between two hollowed-out buildings. A dozen men, real-worlders, loaded up with guns. They were moving in a parody of military style, making the moves they'd learned from watching too many war movies. A dozen guys playing out their Action Hero Schwarzenegger fantasies, swaggering, poking guns here and there, imagining themselves on film, no doubt playing the background music in their heads.

Easy to ridicule them. But their guns were real enough.

One guy seemed to be in charge, a crew-cutted, beer-gutted guy of fifty who looked like the old Navy guy on *Survivor*. He was yelling orders the others occasionally heeded.

"Secure that doorway! Cover that alley!"

Others were marveling aloud: at the castle, at the destruction, at all the cool burning, at the dead men and women. At the dead fairies.

I didn't have the energy to run and hide anymore. I had the energy to breathe, that was about it.

Fortunately, these weren't real soldiers. Some imagined movement down the street set them all to firing wildly and yahooing. Then they were past, and I wasn't dead.

So, Senna was still bringing in more men. How? Wasn't she in the castle? These guys had come up from the countryside to join the party, Johnny-come-latelies to the big party.

The gateway must still be open.

Senna was back out there, out there in the countryside. Why? Had the ring of druid stones held some magic she could use? Was she really back there in that weird little dell? Shouldn't Queen Senna be in the castle?

No, she had to bring in more men. That was

her top priority: She was in a hurry. Why? Because it wasn't over, that's why. She was in a hurry to raise forces. She was expecting trouble. Not from us, we were beat, but from someone.

Merlin? Loki?

The opening of the gateway would send shivers through all the powers of Everworld. Brigid had said that. Loki would know. Ka Anor would know. Huitzilopoctli and Hel and Zeus and Athena and Neptune, they would all know. They were all on the same psychic-magic e-mail list.

But none of them would suspect what was really happening. It wouldn't occur to them any more than it had occurred to us, that the traffic through the gate was Chicago-style: one-way the wrong way.

One way out. One solution, that was clear: Senna had to be stopped. Permanently. The monster I used to date had to be stopped.

No problem, Christopher, I thought. *After all, you have a fairy sword, and what's Senna got, aside from magic powers and a bunch of guys with Kalashnikovs?*

What should I do? What should I do?

Go to the druid stones. Maybe because I could do something to stop her. Or maybe because her enchantment was still strong and I was like some low-level vampire drawn inexorably to the boss vampire. I couldn't even trust my own motives.

And anyway, I knew this: I wasn't going to kill her. Not my thing, you know, killing. It was different if someone was attacking you directly, trying to kill you. Then, in the absence of cops or troops or even a vice principal, you had to defend yourself, no other way. But to lie in wait for Senna and jump out from behind a tree and stick my fairy sword into her? Not me, and not anyone I wanted to hang around with.

Besides, Brigid had said it, right? No one was going to kill Senna.

Still and all, there I was, walking down the too-well-trodden path like a man with a plan. Heading for the dell. So, like I say, I had to question my own motives. Senna's hook was still in me: I was a trout and all she had to do was reel me in and fry me up in the pan.

Out into the countryside. Out into stone-fence and scruffy-tree country. The moon was at the quarter and sliding in and out of the clouds.

"What word, stranger?" a voice asked. A voice in the darkness.

I jumped approximately my own height.

"Peace, brother," the voice said. "Or if not peace, then at least have no fear of me."

When I had swallowed my heart again I peered into the darkness and saw a cloak and a beard. The face was obscured. But the voice was familiar.

"Merlin? Is that you, man?"

"Merlin indeed," he said.

"Yeah? How do I know you're not Senna pretending to be Merlin?"

The wizard laughed softly. "You have begun to learn the ways of Everworld, Christopher."

"Yeah," I said. "But that's not what's up right now, man. What's happening right now is that Everworld is learning the ways of the real world."

He stepped closer. "The witch has opened the gateway. This I know."

"She's importing, not exporting," I said. "Senna's bringing over well-armed guys from the real world. Guns. Lots of guns. You want the short version? Lorg the giant? Dead. MacCool? Dead. Pretty much all the local Fianna are dead. Most of King Cam's fairies? Dead. My friends and Goewynne and Etain and all, I don't know, but Senna's people have burned the town and taken the castle and we're all pretty well screwed. So, what's new with you, Merlin?"

He stroked his beard and considered. "MacCool is dead, then? That is a terrible blow."

I was still not in the mood to hear how great MacCool was. "MacCool didn't like to listen. He thought he knew what was what, and he ended up all full of holes."

Merlin looked up sharply. He looked like he might just decide to put some magic whim-wham on me to teach me not to back-talk him. Then his expression changed.

"Come. I will listen," he said.

XXIV

So we sat down well off the road and damned if Merlin didn't brew up a pot of tea. Made himself a little fire out of damp twigs that shouldn't burn and whipped a little teapot out of his rucksack. It was a Yoda moment. I expected him to start talking backward and moving like a Muppet. "Screwed we are, yes."

But the old wizard didn't get to be an old wizard by being stupid. He clammed up and let me pour out my whole tale of woe. And boy, did I pour. I gave it all to him.

He gave me some tea.

When I was done he did something that endeared him to me: He puffed out his cheeks and shook his head and said, "It looks bad."

Yes, indeedy, it looked bad.

"It may be that the witch's power has

grown too great for me to counter. She has learned much. She has great natural talents. And, of course, her armed men give her very great power."

"But you have it worked out, right?" I said. "I mean, you know how to stop her, right?"

He shook his head and made a slight, rueful smile. "No. Some of what you tell me, I knew already. A mutual friend on the other side, in what you call the real world, had alerted me to hurry."

"Brigid?"

Merlin nodded. "Yes, Brigid has done more for her people than will ever be known. Her powers are limited in the old world, your world, but she has over these many centuries reached across the barrier to defend her people."

"Yeah, we noticed Ireland is doing a little better than the rest of Everworld."

"It is in large part . . ." He stopped. Froze. Seemed to be listening to something far off. "The gateway has closed."

I nodded. "I guess she's brought over all the guys she can find."

Merlin dumped out the last of the tea and made me give him back my cup. Then he stood up. "I can allow us to pass among them, but I do not know the form of them. I do not know their costume."

It took me a minute to get that. "What? You're talking the shape-shifting thing?"

"It is not shape-shifting, my young friend. It is mere illusion. The ignorant call it shape-shifting. The shift is only in their minds. But I must know the look of these armed men in order to allow us to pass among them."

"Us?"

"Us."

"You can do it to me, too?"

"I could make you appear to be a troll or a wolf or a wench," Merlin said, not without some cockiness.

"Yeah? Could you make me appear to be somewhere else?"

No answer.

I sighed. This was a disturbing idea, but I didn't see how I could decently weasel out of it. So I set about telling Merlin how to dress the part of a gun nut.

I drew pictures in the dirt. I painted word pictures. And when it was all done the old man turned himself into an extra from a *Mad Max* movie.

"A little less flamboyant, maybe," I suggested. "The pants should be looser. Longer. The boots are black, not brown."

He adjusted.

"And the gun ... well, it looks too smooth. You need more, I don't know, like slots and stuff. You know what, it'll pass in the dark, and then you can adjust when you see the actual guys."

"Yes, that is what we shall do," he said, again with a not-too-subtle emphasis on "we."

Then he did a kind of cool little trick: He swirled his hand in a tall oval, and there, shimmering, hanging in the air, was a mirror. In the mirror, a reasonably convincing version of a skinhead. I ran my hand over my scalp. Weird. I could feel hair, but in the mirror I saw shaved scalp.

In my hands I cradled a gun I couldn't actually feel. Air gun.

"A tattoo," I suggested. "Here, on my arm. A dragon swirled around a Confederate battle flag and the words 'Born to Raise Hell.'"

The tattoo appeared, although the flag in question was closer to the British flag.

"Good enough. Now what?"

"We wait," Merlin said. "They are coming."

Sure enough, when I looked down the road I saw a ragged line of torches.

"Shouldn't we hide?"

"No. We should merely be silent."

They came on, and we stood there in plain view, but apparently invisible. They came on, maybe twenty men, all armed to the teeth and favoring the camouflage look. They were singing as they went, and I kid you not, they were singing "Dixie."

"Dixie." A bunch of guys from Chicago, for God's sake, singing "Dixie" like they were somehow the natural heirs of Robert E. Lee and Stonewall Jackson, the jackasses.

And there was Senna at their head. Senna but not Senna. This was an enhanced Senna. Senna on steroids. The action figure of Senna. She had turned herself into the Frank Frazetta version of Senna: rippling muscles and costume straight out of some maladjusted comic-book reader's sadomasochistic fantasy. She was swaggering in a very un-Senna sort of way. Wearing a sword and a winged opera helmet. A Valkyrie, I realized. We'd seen the actual Valkyries, and she had copied their look.

I almost giggled. I mean, come on: Even in Everworld there should be some kind of a limit on fashion choices.

But I guess she was giving the troops what they wanted: some overblown, Edgar Rice Burroughs heroine. Big Babes on Mars.

She came nearer, lit by high-held torches, keeping step with the shouted, defiant song, high on her own power, pumped both physically and psychologically.

The illusory gun I was holding changed subtly as Merlin saw some of the real thing.

Senna came level with us. A frown. A look of uncertainty in her eyes. She felt our presence. She was going to kill me. She was going, I swear to God, going to kill us, going to see us, reach right over and kill me.

I held my breath. Glanced nervously at Merlin. He was watching Senna, eyes glittering, focused. He didn't look too relaxed himself.

Then Senna shook off her doubts and marched on. The column passed by and at the end, we stepped onto the road joining the column. We were visible now. The guy immediately ahead of us turned and gave us a suspicious look from under the brim of his Wehrmacht cap. Merlin smiled at the guy and the guy went kind of blank and then nodded, like we'd known each other all along.

Merlin went to work with shocking efficiency. He stepped up behind Wehrmacht Cap and calmly cut his throat.

I had to cover my mouth to stifle the surprised yelp.

Merlin bent over the body, yanked the guy's Uzi away, and handed it to me. "I take it we need this instrument?" he said.

I nodded and tried not to think about what I'd

gotten myself into. "I need the guy's ammo belt, too," I said.

Now I was carrying a real weapon, not an illusion. That was comforting. Not real comforting, but all in all, if you're going to end up in a gun fight you want to avoid carrying an imaginary weapon. Pointing your finger and going, "Bang! Bang!" is not all that effective.

We marched on our rollicking way: 'Roid-Senna in the lead, Merlin and me in the rear, and in between twenty or so living proofs that white people aren't really superior.

Through the countryside. Into the town, mostly charred rubble now. Over the bodies. Up the hill to the castle. In the gate.

And there it was, the scene Senna must have dreamed about for a long time: The courtyard was filled with her soldiers, all cheering wildly at her entrance. They lined the walls of the courtyard and the tops of the walls, poised atop the crenellations, many if not most holding torches. How many? At least fifty, seventy-five with our contingent added. It seemed like more. All armed to the teeth.

In the center of the courtyard a dozen people stood staggering under the weight of massive chains. David, Jalil, King Camulos, Fios, Goewynne, a handful of druids I didn't know, and Etain.

The chains were looped around legs and waists, over shoulders, around necks. Here and there massive, primitive locks had been placed. The chain links were each big enough to stick your hand through. The chains weighed a ton. Etain was on her knees, unable to carry the weight, her head bowed low. Her clothes were ripped, shredded. Goewynne had been hit. Her face was bruised. The king was badly wounded, clutching his side, blood seeping from a gut wound. A blue druid, a young guy with an incongruously full beard and strange green eyes, was trying to help stem the flow of royal blood.

David was a mess. His own mother wouldn't have recognized him. He'd been professionally beaten. One eye was closed by a knot the size of a lemon. Jalil wasn't much better off.

April was nowhere to be seen. That was the worst of it, because although seeing them like this made me burn, not seeing April, not knowing what had happened to her, or was happening to her, that was worse still.

I felt Merlin's hand on my arm. Restraining me. He looked at me with eyes that were not his own, and shook his head slowly.

I unclenched my fists. Forced myself to breathe. Loosened the finger that had wrapped around the Uzi's trigger.

"Silence!" Senna roared.

The yelping and hallooing and yeehahing and sieg-heiling calmed down. An expectant pause.

"Hello, David. Hello, Jalil," she said in a sneering voice intended to reach most of her troops.

No answer. The crowd leaned forward expectantly. They wanted to see what the Great One was going to do. I guessed that most of these guys didn't really know what they'd gotten themselves into, or who, exactly, they were following.

"Nothing to say, David?" Senna demanded.

David just looked at her.

Keith stepped up behind him and nailed him in the kidneys with his rifle butt. He went down, gasping for breath, an involuntary whimper of pain escaping. But then he levered himself back up, fighting the pain and the weight of his chains.

"Where are the other two?" Senna demanded in a hiss of a voice.

The question was directed at a guy I hadn't noticed before: a skinhead wearing a muscle T-shirt over plenty of muscle.

Muscle Shirt looked uncertain. "What other two, Great One?"

"April and Christopher," she said. "Where are they?"

"The uh . . . the blond guy, that's Christopher, right?" Muscle Shirt stammered. "He got killed. He's . . . the body is right over, you know, Great One, with the other bodies."

"Bring it here. I want to see it," Senna ordered.

This ought to be good, I thought. A bunch of toadies raced off to rummage through the grisly heap of bodies by the gate. I was pretty sure they weren't going to find my body.

Senna waited impatiently, staring holes through Muscle Shirt. The flunkies returned empty-handed.

Senna drew her lips back in a feral snarl I'd never seen before. "You let Christopher escape. Well, that's okay, I'll let that go. He's irrelevant. But April . . . that's a different matter entirely. Where is my favorite half sister?"

Muscle Shirt looked around like someone else might come forward to take the blame. Oddly enough, no one volunteered. I spotted Keith in the crowd. He was carefully looking down at the ground.

"No April," Senna said regretfully. "And yet, my orders were clear: At all costs get the four real-worlders. Despite this, I see only half of them here. Well, half a failure earns half a punishment."

She waved her Demi Moore arms very theatrically, and instantly Muscle Shirt's body burst into flames. No, only half. He burned only on his left side. Burned as if someone had poured lighter fluid all over him and struck a match.

He screamed and flapped at himself as every glittering eye gazed on in horror and fascination. Muscle Shirt's flesh crisped and peeled like pork cracklings in the barbecue.

Senna was burning a man alive.

Then, as suddenly as it had begun, it was over. Muscle Shirt quivered, shook, whimpered as he touched the burned flesh that now, magically, was whole and sound and unharmed again.

The burning had been an illusion, but no less hideous for that fact. A display by the Great One. A little lesson on who held the power. And her boys loved it. They were horrified and sickened and scared peeless, but they loved it just the same.

David had watched the whole thing stonily. Jalil's face was a mask of indifference. Etain had raised her head as much as she could, but let it sink back down under the weight of her chains. King Camulos was too gone even to glare, he was bleeding out. The blue druid eased him to the ground and knelt beside him. Goewynne tried to go to her husband, but Keith yanked her back by her hair.

Senna owned the crowd, that was for sure. Nothing like a display of casual brutality to really wow this particular crowd. She strode her newly muscular way up to David.

"General Davideus," she said. "You've been out-generaled." She laughed at that. Laughed. Senna, a person who pretty much never laughed.

She was way off the deep end of the pier. She was channeling Mussolini at this point: strutting, posturing, flexing her illusory muscles, sticking out her rock-hard chest. She was playing to the crowd, camping it up, making them love her.

"David Levin!" she yelled, pointing an accusing finger at David. She'd placed extra emphasis on the "Levin," and through the crowd went the murmured response, "Jew."

"David was once my tool," she announced, clenching her fist. "But he defied me. And now he will suffer as all who defy me suffer."

Anticipation. Excitement. Oooh, the good stuff was still to come.

She turned to Jalil, and now the faked hatred she'd exposed toward David was replaced by real hatred.

"Still the unbeliever, Jalil?" she mocked. "Still

think you're going to dissect me, take me apart, outsmart me?"

Jalil remained silent. I knew him well enough to know he was scared, but damned if he showed it.

"Pray to me, Jalil," Senna whispered. "Down on your knees and pray to me. Beg me for your life, and I'll let you keep it."

"I don't think so, Senna," he said.

"I think you will," she said. "You know, Jalil, I think your hands are very, very dirty."

Jalil looked blank, then slowly at first, then faster, he began rubbing his hands, rubbing at them with imaginary soap. He rubbed and rubbed, twisted them, worried them, scratched and clawed at the backs of his hands.

Blood began to flow.

"Jalil has a little problem. Did you know that, David? Jalil just can't seem to get clean. What's it called, Jalil? Obsessive-compulsive?"

"Stop it," David snapped.

"Jalil's a sick, sick boy. He tries so hard to be all brain, but his brain is sick. Sick and dirty, right, Jalil?"

"I said stop it," David said.

"No, I don't think so," Senna said and giggled as Jalil became more frantic. His hands were bloody, his nails clawing, and now tears rolled down his face as the crowd laughed and hooted, unsure what they were seeing, but glad to see the black man cry and bleed.

"I'll make him claw himself down to the bone," Senna said to David. "He'll clean himself to death."

"Do something," I muttered to Merlin.

"This is not the time," he whispered. "Something will happen soon, and then the time will be ripe. Soon! He approaches. I sense his approach."

"He? Who he?"

No answer.

"Jalil, oh, Jalil," Senna mocked in a singsong voice. "Your face is dirty now. Filthy!"

Jalil shuddered, tried to resist, then began slowly to scrub and finally to claw at his face.

"You sick bitch!" someone yelled.

That someone, to my great horror, was me.

Senna spun on her heels, and for a sweet moment I saw fear in her eyes. The tyrant's natural, instinctive fear of defiance.

"Who said that?" she shrieked.

"You really must learn patience," Merlin snapped in an undertone. Then, without missing a beat, he yelled, "He said it!" and pointed his illusory finger at an unoffending creep standing beside me.

"No!" the creep yelled, but way too late.

Senna aimed a finger at him and he burst into flame. I backpedaled, everyone did, backed away as the guy screamed and writhed, and I knew deep down that this time it was no illusion.

I could smell it this time.

He fell to his knees, a living torch. His gun fell from his grip and I snatched it up like I was trying to save valuable hardware from being wasted. It was hot to the touch.

Senna's mad, distorted face glowed in the flames.

Bang! Bang!

Not me, not anyone firing a gun, the reports were from cartridges in the dead man's ammo belt fired off by the heat of the flames. Everyone scattered. The guy had loaded magazines all over, maybe a hundred rounds, and Senna, who was not only a complete whack job, but not real bright when it came to weapons, had lit up what amounted to a walking ammunition dump.

The Sennites up on the walls crouched behind stone. Everyone down below bolted for cover. It was a kitchen full of cockroaches when someone turns on a light.

Bang! Bang! Bang!

The bullets went off randomly, in groups of two or three, in singles, unpredictable. Merlin and I had run with everyone else and we were behind a stone well. Only the chained prisoners and Senna remained exposed, and David was yelling, "Get down!"

Etain and Goewynne were already down, but now the druids and the king dropped, too. One of the druids was too slow. A bullet caught him in the leg.

But, of course, bullets fired without benefit of a barrel were less dangerous. The explosion was not confined so they were dangerous only at close range.

I saw David slipping out of his chains. He must have beat the lock already because he sloughed off the weight without too much trouble and was now grabbing Jalil, pulling Jalil's clawing hands away from his face.

Senna looked like the visiting head of the school board addressing the assembly where someone has lit a stink bomb. She was outraged and confused at losing control. She was furious and unsure of where to direct her rage, what with the fact that she herself was responsible for this particular fiasco.

One thing was sure: Senna had to go. Senna was loony. The human race was going to have to get along without her.

I did what I never wanted to do: I leveled my rifle, took shaky aim, and squeezed the trigger.

Nothing.

The safety!

I fumbled madly, looking for the safety. Was that it, or wasn't the thing even cocked? What was . . . there, that had to be the safety.

I clicked it, but a hand was already wrapped around the barrel, forcing it down.

No man would take Senna's life. That's what Brigid had said.

I looked up into Senna's manic face. "Who are you?" she demanded. Of course, she couldn't yet see through Merlin's disguise of me.

She put her free hand on my face, almost caressing, and I felt all the anger, all the determination slip away, disappear behind a bank of fog that rolled into my brain.

"It's just me, Christopher," I said.

CHAPTER
XXVI

"Christopher, of course," she said. Then, raising her voice to a shout, she yelled, "Come and take this garbage away!"

I was confused for a moment because I thought she was talking about me, and she couldn't be talking about me because I loved her, I loved her and served her, and always would.

But no, to my deep relief she was talking about the dead man, the burned corpse who had, at last, slowed his rate of fire.

A couple of her soldiers came running, eager to please, scared to disappoint, but leery about grabbing onto a charcoal briquette studded with unfired rounds.

There was a bang and a yelp of pain, but they managed after some confusion to throw a rope around the remains and drag him off at a run toward the gate.

The cowering minions resurfaced, laughing with relief.

"All we need is April now," Senna said, caressing my face. "And, of course, master Merlin. He must be very nearby. Only he could have disguised you so effectively."

I was all set to point Merlin out, but the wizard was no longer where I'd last seen him. Senna noticed my puppy-dog eagerness and frustration and patted my head almost affectionately.

"No, no, never fret, Christopher: He's shifted himself again, no doubt. But we'll find him, won't we? We'll find the wizard yet."

"We'll get him," I said. "We'll get April, too."

Senna looked sharply at me. "Do you know where she is?"

"No," I said. And yet, at that same moment, a flash of memory, an image. Blue. Green eyes. A strange beard.

I tried to put it together in my head, tried to make sense of it. The answer would please Senna, and pleasing Senna was the point. I tried to focus, tried to think, but it was as if someone else was in my head, blocking my every attempt.

Senna turned away. Time to rally the troops.

"Brave soldiers of the New Order," she cried. "A wizard is among us. None other than Merlin the Magnificent. He is passing as one of you. But you know who you are. Each of you is known to at least a few others. Look around at your companions, and point out the soldier who is unknown. Find the outsider."

Muttering, suspicious looks, yelling back and forth. Just the kind of assignment to appeal to this crowd: Find the outsider.

"There!" a voice cried finally. "That one. No one knows him." It was Keith, pointing triumphantly.

"What the hell are you talking about? It's me, John Loboda. Terry, you know me! Al, you know me."

But Terry and Al shook their heads. "That ain't Big John. I've never seen that guy."

"Kill him!" Senna snapped.

The sound of guns blazing and the victim fell. He fell and as he died his appearance changed. Senna ran forward eagerly, expecting to see Merlin's bullet-riddled corpse.

Instead she saw what had to be the actual John Loboda.

A laugh. Loud and sustained and mocking. An old man's laugh. Merlin's voice.

Senna flushed red. She realized too late: Merlin

had altered John Loboda's face, just as he had disguised me.

"You wanted to play Merlin's game, witch," the wizard said from nowhere in particular. "Your move."

Senna was definitely freaked. So were her troops. This wasn't in the script. Mighty Senna the Great One was getting yanked. She'd just been tricked into ordering a faithful follower shot. That didn't sit well with the other faithful followers, and Senna knew it. It's okay to punish failure. This was a whole other thing.

And at that moment a voice cried, "Hey! Hey! Something's happening down in the town."

It was a lookout, high on the walls.

"What is it?" Keith yelled back, assuming the mantle of lieutenant, I guess.

"It's like . . . there's a bunch of guys coming," the lookout cried. "And some kind of big, I mean, freaking huge-ass wolf."

In my dopey, bewitched state of mind, I didn't click. Didn't figure out who the wolf was, who it had to be.

But Senna did.

"Fenrir," she whispered. "Yes. Come, Fenrir, come, Loki, I await you."

"He comes, witch," Merlin's voice-from-nowhere shouted. "Great Loki is come for you at last."

Jalil started talking, loud, persuasive. "You poor dumb fools, you don't know what she's gotten you into. Loki is coming. He's a god. And his son, Fenrir. You know what Fenrir is? He's a wolf the size of an elephant. She's gotten you all killed. You followed this psycho and she's gotten you all killed. Look! She's lost control. She can't handle Merlin and Loki at once. Fenrir is going to chew you up and crap you out."

"Silence!" Senna screamed. But her brain was going, wheels spinning, too busy to waste time torturing Jalil.

"Loki comes," Merlin intoned helpfully. "You may still escape, witch. Surrender yourself to me."

"What do we do, Great One?" Keith demanded.

"You're all dead," Jalil crowed. "You think she's going to lead you? She's some head case of a girl from the North Shore, how stupid are you?"

"Great One," Keith pressed.

My own slow, bewitched brain clicked. A druid with green eyes? April! April the actress. April. Senna would be so happy to find April.

"Senna," I said. "I know —"

Senna pressed her hands against her temples, squeezing. "Shut up. Obey me!"

"Everyone shut up!" Keith reiterated savagely.

"Forget the wizard, I'll deal with him later," Senna said. "Man the walls. Raise the drawbridge.

Close the gate. We have a battle to fight!" That last was in a roar, her face up to the crowds atop the walls.

The troops bellowed their relieved approval. This they understood. They were going to get a chance to shoot some people. Cool.

Could they really stop Loki and Fenrir? Could bullets kill a god?

"Here they come!" the lookout yelled. "There's, like — man, that wolf is huge. And the guys aren't human."

"Trolls!" Merlin's mocking voice cried helpfully. "Living stone."

"You're all dead," Jalil said, keeping up his trash-talking monologue. I expected him to start with "no batter, no batter" next.

"You'll be lucky to be dead. Loki may give you to his daughter, Hel," Jalil said. "You'll be buried alive up to your necks. You'll be cobblestones for her to walk over."

"I think I'll kill you right now," Keith screamed at Jalil, spit flying.

"Your Great One hasn't given you that order," David intervened quickly. "A soldier follows orders."

"There's hundreds of them," the lookout cried.

Keith put his face up to Jalil's. "Great One," he said, "let me kill this one. Right now."

David sloughed off the last of his chains, free, and slammed into Keith. Keith hit the ground, swung his gun up, and caught David a brutal blow under the chin. David dropped.

The ground shook like the opening rumble of an earthquake. Something big was knocking on the castle door. Gunfire blazed from the wall above. Everyone on the wall was firing, a deafening din.

Another massive blow and the castle gate blew inward, matchsticks and kindling.

Fenrir leaped through, enormous, shaggy, and gray. He shouldered into the castle and let loose a roar that would have knocked the glass out of every window, if there'd been any glass.

Trolls shoved around him, under his legs, rushing to get inside the castle. A dozen or more, thick, squat, living-stone creatures with hornless rhino heads. They swung curved swords but had no targets.

The men on the battlements shifted, turned and directed their fire down at Loki's son. The wolf-god was impossible to miss. Hundreds of rounds hit his neck, his head.

Fenrir bellowed in rage and agony. When he opened his mouth, blue blood gushed through his teeth. Still the men fired and now the wolf

was lost, snapping at the air, bellowing, dangerous but helpless to reach or stop his tormentors.

A bestial cry of triumph went up from the men
and Fenrir fell.

The trolls quavered, unsure. Then, in shock,
they broke and ran.

Keith stood over a beaten David. Leveled his
weapon at him, and my own mind, my treason-
ous, bewitched mind thought, *Yes, do it!*

I glanced at the blue druid with the incongruous beard and green eyes. April. King Camulos
was dead at her feet. She started toward Keith.

I yelled, "It's her! It's April!"

Senna spun, her attention suddenly riveted on
me. "Where? Where?"

I started to point. Jalil staggered forward, using
the weight of his chains to bear Keith down. The
two of them fell in a heap. But Jalil wasn't focusing on Keith. He twisted around and stuck out
one hand, one clawed, bloody hand to April.

April leaped, grabbed what Jalil had given her,
and in a flash I knew what it was: Jalil's Swiss
Army knife. The tiny little knife with the two-
inch blade that had been replaced by the Coo-
Hatch.

I raised my gun, aimed it at April. April leaped
at Senna. Some unseen force pushed my gun bar-

rel up as I fired. Merlin! The gun kicked in my hands and a line of bullets passed over April's head.

But the noise drew Senna's gaze to me, to me, away from April, away from the Coo-Hatch blade.

April stabbed.

The blade went in like a red-hot ice pick in a pound of butter.

Senna grabbed her chest, laughed in disbelief, stared at the blue druid, and now, now too late, saw the familiar green eyes.

"You," she sobbed.

Senna fell backward. No longer the illusory Senna of rippling muscles, the Valkyrie Senna. Just Senna, the girl I used to date.

I knew she was dead. Knew it beyond any doubt: Her hold over me snapped, ceased, a light switch turned off.

Keith was freeing himself. I ran over, kicked his gun away, and drew down on him.

"You better shoot me," Keith said to me. "Because if you don't, I'll sure as hell kill you."

I shook my head. "I think we've had about enough killing." Then I slammed my rifle butt into his chin and he went down like a sandbag. "Of course, ass-kicking, that's different: Still have some room for that."

I looked at Senna. Senna the witch. Senna the

gateway. Senna the whole reason for us even being in this nuthouse. She didn't look like too much now.

April was frozen, unable to move. She was just staring. Her half sister's blood was all over her hand.

I don't think any of us would have known what to do next but for Merlin, who appeared beside me.

"We must leave," he said. "The battle still rages, but Loki has lost. Soon these men will turn their attention back to us. There is a tunnel that leads from the keep, under the moat. It is the only way."

"I will not leave my husband," Goewynne said.

"You will, Goewynne," Merlin said. "You are still a queen. Your people have need of you."

I knelt beside Etain. "Come on, we have to get out of here. Hold still."

I laid the lock of her chains on the ground, made sure she was turned away, and shot the lock. I extricated her from her chains and helped her to her feet. But Etain couldn't walk.

I picked her up, like some kind of romance novel hero, I picked her up, and followed Merlin.

Goewynne stayed behind to kneel by her husband and kiss his forehead.

We left the castle in the hands of the now-

leaderless Sennites. We left Senna lying in the
dust. No one retrieved Jalil's knife.

Goewynne came and took April's hand. She led
April away. April was gone to us. Jalil helped support David. Merlin led the way, and I hugged
Etain close and wondered, as each of us was wondering, how, with the gateway dead, how we
would ever get home.

EVER WORLD

#XII

ENTERTAIN THE END

And I ran, head down, out to the street. Tore down the block to my car, fumbled wildly for the keys, then locked myself in and flipped down the visor on the passenger side. Looked into the mirror there.

Half a face looked back at me. A flickering and my left eye returned, went away, came back.

I watched, fascinated, until my entire face came back into view. Then I leaned my head against the steering wheel.

It was finally happening. Real-word April was leaving home.

After a minute I started the car and began to drive toward Christopher's house. I needed to tell him it was finally happening to me. Then I would look for Jalil. . . .

I drove to Christopher's house. A block away I

saw flashing lights and knew they were for him. I parked a few houses down, ran past the faces peeping curiously from windows and the nosy woman standing in an open doorway.

One ambulance, one police car. Great. The way my day was going, Detectives Costello and Hayes would come cruising around the corner next.

Just as I reached the Hitchcocks' lawn, the front door opened. Two paramedics wheeled a gurney over the doorsill and lifted it down the few stairs to the front walk. Christopher's father stood in the open door and watched his son being wheeled away.

"Christopher!" I raced to his side and gripped the metal edge of the gurney. Walked along with the paramedics who seemed strangely disturbed and nervous. "What happened?"

"Boys, how about you let me talk to my friend here for a minute, okay?"

The paramedics stopped wheeling. *Since when is a patient in charge?* I thought.

Christopher didn't look sick. In fact, he looked kind of — happy. "Well, April, Mom caught a glimpse of me without my shirt on. Didn't know she'd come into my room to put away some laundry."

"You mean . . ."

"Take a look." Christopher yanked the sheet

covering him from the leather restraints. The paramedics stepped back.

I sucked in a breath. "I see. Or, I don't see. Whatever."

Christopher was mostly not there. No chest, but some stomach. One shoulder.

He leered. "Want to see what else is missing?"

"No. Oh, my God, Christopher." I leaned close to his ear. "How are you going to explain this! What are you going to do!"

"Keep my mouth shut," he said. "What else can I do? And you're looking a little, uh, pale, too, right now. If you know what I mean."

"I started to fade out at dinner. I was on a date and the guy freaked. I came right over to see you."

"Yeah, well, thanks. I guess. Look, I suggest you get home, now. Go in the back way, don't let your mother see you. Or we're gonna be roomies in intensive care."

"Okay. Christopher, the police came to my house today," I said in a rush. "They wanted to know about Senna and David. They know I'm not telling the truth. I . . ."

"Don't wait up for me, April," Christopher said, as if he hadn't heard me at all, a strange, spacey smile on his face. "I think you might be wasting your time. . . ."